I Am Sovereign

NICOLA BARKER

I Am Sovereign

WILLIAM HEINEMANN: LONDON

1 3 5 7 9 10 8 6 4 2

William Heinemann
20 Vauxhall Bridge Road
London SW1V 2SA

William Heinemann is part of the Penguin Random House group
of companies whose addresses can be found at
global.penguinrandomhouse.com.

Copyright © Nicola Barker 2019

First published by William Heinemann in 2019

www.penguin.co.uk

A CIP catalogue record for this book is available from the British Library.

ISBN 9781785152269

Typeset in 12.82/16.57 pts Baskerville
by Integra Software Services Pvt. Ltd, Pondicherry

Printed and bound in Great Britain by Clays Ltd, Elcograf S.p.A.

Penguin Random House is committed to a sustainable future for our
business, our readers and our planet. This book is made from Forest
Stewardship Council® certified paper.

For Patrick Hargadon
and his trademark luminously bright white socks

Where is the life we have lost in living?
T.S. Eliot

1.

GO, LOCAL SPORTS TEAM, GO!

Charles can't get started. He has written an email to the help-desk at *Silencing the Inner Critic* telling Richard Grannon that he can't get started and wondering if there's anything in particular that he can do to rectify this parlous situation. He honestly doesn't know why he can't get started. When he thinks about how angry he is with himself (because of how he can't get started) he begins to flashback and remember how his dad always used to say that he was a pathetic piece of crap who would never amount to anything. Next he feels this unbearable 'constricted feeling' in his chest, and, in exquisite conjunction with that unbearable constriction – like a cowboy cantering along, determinedly, beside a demented heifer – an equivalently overwhelming urge to go online and surf the algorithms and buy a book or – better still – an audio book called something like: *Living Your Unlived Life.*

He imagines listening to this audiobook at night on his laptop while he's sleeping – or on his nifty, brand-new, clean-white, kinda-space-cube-y, wall-mounted CD player (if he can burn a CD on his brand-new-as-yet-unboxed CD burner) which seems to have no automatic stop mechanism (the reviewers on Amazon were definitely niggled/bemused by this) so is essentially permanently on repeat – and ... and ... yes, and the positive messages will seep gently and painlessly into his unconscious mind ... or ... or his *conscious* mind (more likely), when he's *not* managing to sleep, because he actually *cannot* sleep, because he is so frustrated by the fact that he can't get started and he truly fucking hates himself. He fucking hates himself for this blatant sign of his manifold cowardice and impotence and ineffectualness and weakness.

Just. *Can't.* Get. Started.

Never. Quite. Got. Started.

My. Whole. Damn. *Life.*

This is his Toxic Super-Ego at work. Surely? The Toxic Super-Ego tells Charles that he is a pathetic piece of crap just like his dad always said he was. The Toxic Super-Ego is the Parent voice. It's his dad's voice. It is constantly at work within him – hectoring him, lecturing him, pointing the finger. Finding fault.

Plenty to find fault with here, kiddo ...

'WAH! NO! Stop it! *Stop* it, Toxic Super-Ego!' Charles immediately counters. 'I'm calling you out, see? I'm wise to your games now! I know who you are! I know what you do!'

In the Introductory Module which Charles has only watched half of because he suddenly felt terrified and overwhelmed and tired – *tired*, just so ludicrously, deliriously *tired* – Richard Grannon stood majestically in front of a whiteboard wearing a newly pressed blue shirt and calmly outlined the role of the Toxic Super-Ego. The Toxic Super-Ego was sitting (Grannon drew a little cartoon with his trusty marker pen) in its own small bath of 'toxic shame'.

Grannon is funny and handsome and 'buff' and Charles finds it difficult to believe that Grannon was also an unholy screw-up a mere two years ago. *Two years.* Before he cured himself.

He and Richard Grannon are approximately the same age.
There is still hope.

Although there is already something about this picture that doesn't entirely add up. If a person is truly, *authentically* an unholy screw-up then how the hell do they still manage to hold down a job as a life-coach/therapist and teach high-level martial arts and do a series of other remarkably cool and interesting things like becoming an NLP Master Practitioner and living in the Far East and having an encyclopedic knowledge of Important Cultural Moments in both fiction and film while owning a giant, blonde dog which lollops about shedding hair and stealing socks?

?

Who looks after this beloved dog while Grannon's kicking back in the Far East?

Huh?

If Grannon doesn't take good care of his dog, how do you know you can trust him to take proper care of YOU?!

Charles has inherited a hairless Sphynx cat called Morpheus and the cat refuses to either eat or drink if Charles goes away on a trip. When Charles went to an uncle's funeral (not a real uncle but a real funeral) in Wick for three days the cat had to be rushed to the vet and put on a drip.
Fucking co-dependent fucking *cat*.

This is your Toxic Super-Ego at play, Charles tells himself. Grannon warned you that the Toxic Super-Ego (TSE) would start trying to undermine and ridicule 'the process'. The TSE doesn't want to be eclipsed.
You are AT WAR with the TSE. The TSE is a vicious rogue element – a terrorist – which has secretly hijacked your brain. It is bloated beyond all recognition – like a degenerate mid-seventies Elvis. It is marching around vaingloriously – like a psychological Napoleon in a ridiculous cocked-hat. It has short man syndrome.

But remember – *remember!* – that you don't want it to know you are AT WAR with it. Too risky. You want to sneak up on it and catch it unawares. To set a cunning trap. To approach it, with stealth, and then ...

to *POUNCE.*

Because ... *shhh!*

*YOU ARE NOT STRONG ENOUGH TO DECLARE OUTRIGHT WAR ON THE TSE! IT WILL CALMLY AND SYSTEMATICALLY PULVERISE AND DEGRADE AND HUMILIATE YOU IF IT CATCHES WIND THAT ANYTHING – **ANYTHING** – UNTOWARD IS UNDER WAY. BECAUSE THAT'S SIMPLY WHO IT IS AND WHAT IT DOES.*

IT IS POWERFUL.
IT IS CUNNING.
*IT *gasp!* **HATES** YOU.*

Beware!

Oh balls. Oh *balls*, Charles thinks. If *only* I could get to grips with the course, watch it *from start to finish* (YES! The Holy Grail!) instead of just dipping in and dipping out. If only I could muster a sense of ... of order, of connectedness, of *coherence*. If only I could marshal my *wayward spirit*. Then – only then – might I finally be able to come to grips with the

6

malign influence the Toxic Super-Ego is exerting on my every waking thought and feeling and breath and impulse.

Charles feels so ... so *disparate*.

Desperate?

No.

Disparate.

'I suppose the important detail here is that he – or she – didn't actually break in,' Avigail murmurs, 'she just tried. She tried but she failed.'
Avigail looks at Charles. Charles is holding a pop-corn maker (retailing at £14.95 excl. p&p) which is still boxed and which he is trying to give to the prospective purchaser, a ferocious-seeming Chinese woman called Wang Shu who seems to speak no English. Wang Shu is barely through the front door. Wang Shu's interpreter is her dumpy daughter who has her right arm encased – wrist to elbow – in slightly grimy gauze. The daughter is called Ying

Yue. Ying Yue has emphatically assured Avigail (on Wang Shu's behalf – and insofar as Ying Yue *can* be emphatic, which isn't very far) that Wang Shu will not be put off by the sheer amount of *stuff* clogging up Charles's small property, because the property number just happens to be 8, which is highly propitious in Chinese culture.

Charles lives in the centre of Llandudno in a curious house which has no real, independent character and seems more like the back end of a giant office space (a dark corner for designated parking, drains and growling air-conditioning filters) or possibly even the unkempt kitchens of a large but seedy hotel. There is no front. It is all rear. Small windows. It's on a grimy side street close to the seafront. There is no garden. There is hardly any pavement. He inherited the property from his mother. His mother (Branimira) had worked for thirty years as a veterinary nurse in Conwy – after arriving in Wales from her native Bulgaria in 1964 – even though she was always allergic to both hair and fur.

Hair *and* fur.

(In fact hair and fur aren't actually, *qualitatively* different, they're just alternate words for the same keratin-based substance. It's the proteins – Can f 1 and Fel d 1 – which are released in the dog's saliva and the cat's saliva/skin that provoke allergic responses.)

Charles's mother was not a home-body or a consumerist. Charles's mother was made of sterner stuff. Charles's mother lived at a high altitude – a lofty attitude. Charles's mother lived a life of the spirit.

Charles's mother *LOVED TO GIVE.*

Without inhibition.

But not to Charles. No. No. No. Not to Charles.

Mainly to the helpless, the dispossessed and animals (including insects and birds).

Then to Charles.
All the left-overs. The scraps. The hard rind. The soggy remnants.

The mess was one thing, Avigail thought, but the gulls – the *gulls* – which nested on every, single chimney pot on Trevor Street and shat everywhere. *Everywhere.* And the young – the fledglings – just crashing about and mewing incessantly and getting squashed on the road.

Charles had also tried to give this same boxed popcorn maker to the previous person she brought to view the place – tried – and yet still didn't quite manage to part with it. The previous viewer was called Malc and loved popcorn.

This is the problem.
This is one of the problems with selling the property.
This is one of the problems with Charles.

Avigail has tried (politely, yet strenuously – if these two adverbs can ever really be believably applied in conjunction) to encourage Charles to go out during viewings – to vacate the property, to leave everything in her perfectly capable hands – because he is tall and awkward and sarcastic and ungainly and he makes the house seem even smaller than it actually is. But he won't. She thinks he's fearful about leaving his stuff unguarded. He is a hoarder.

He is very protective of his stuff, while pretending
– to himself, at least, but he's not fooling anyone –
that he can't wait to get rid of it – the *burden* of it –
and to move on with his life. Hence the whole silly
performance with the popcorn maker.

Oh yes.
Avigail is perfectly wise to Charles's little games.
She can see that it's all just a pathetic charade.

Charles wears ironic T-shirts. Today's reads: *Go,
Local Sports Team, Go!*
He is chronically shy but he still somehow con-
spires to over-share. He is very happy to talk about
the attempted burglary that took place over twelve
years ago when his mother was living alone in the
property.
Oh my goodness! The attempted burglary! The
broken window! The dropped knife!

Ying Yue doesn't even *want* the popcorn maker. Ying
Yue doesn't like popcorn. She has sensitive teeth so
finds corn problematic; the way it pretends to be fluffy
and then a nasty piece of kernel sneaks up into the
tight gaps between your molars and … and … *ouch.*

But Wang Shu has a keen eye for an opportunity. Always. Ying Yue hopes that Wang Shu won't embarrass them both by snatching the popcorn maker from Charles and charging off with it. Second-hand goods are not considered propitious in Chinese culture, but Wang Shu is one of life's great pragmatists. Wang Shu was raised by a group of kindly but brutish prostitutes in Guangzhou. Her sullen, calculating father was their pimp. Okay. Not even their pimp. He was the sullen, calculating half-brother of their sullen, calculating pimp. Wang Shu never had a mother − or nobody she could officially *call* a mother − just a succession of 'aunties' who sincerely tried to do their best for her (and failed). This is why Wang Shu is an obsessive deal maker. She has always made deals. It's how she understands love.

Wang Shu is constantly talking on the phone in Chinese to various important contacts back home. Making deals. At this very moment, Wang Shu is on the phone talking in Chinese.

Ying Yue grew up in North Wales and cannot speak Chinese. At least she doesn't feel like she can speak Chinese. Perhaps she can. Yes. Perhaps she can. But she doesn't feel like she can, somehow. It's like not remembering that you can ride a bike until you are seated on the saddle and then you pick up your feet and suddenly, instinctively, start to pedal ...

Ying Yue has never owned a bike or ridden on one. It is a dream of hers that one day – one day – she will ride on a bicycle. As she stands in the hallway she rests her hand on the saddle of Charles's late mother's bicycle that is parked there: it's a heavy, old-fashioned, deep blue British Roadster with a wonderful, brown sprung saddle, full mudguards, a sturdy chain case, useful kickstand and bell.

Ying Yue is twenty-seven years old and has never really been given the opportunity to relax, to unwind and to play. She is – and has always been – on perpetual guard; on watch duty for Wang Shu. Because she has never been able to let loose and have fun in her day-to-day life, she gently rebels (although she would never see it in these terms – she is not remotely rebellious) by constantly playing funny little games inside her mind. Ying Yue is extremely earnest. On the surface, at least, Ying Yue is a perfect picture of submissive conformity. Of polite obedience. Ying Yue always takes everything very seriously – aside from herself, that is.

As long as she can remember, Ying Yue – the true daughter of Wang Shu – has been completely grown up and burdened by a huge number of weighty responsibilities. Even as a toddler she worried about – and felt the burden of – Wang Shu's immense import and majesty.

Ying Yue is Wang Shu's mirror. She reflects Wang Shu back at her (but a nicer version of Wang Shu. A better, more contained and more obliging version of Wang Shu). That is Ying Yue's job – to be a mirror.

The name Wang Shu belonged originally to the god who drives the carriage of the moon. The moon, to the Chinese, represents gentleness and tenderness, so the god who drives the carriage of the moon is a renowned and important figure. Ying Yue's name, on the other hand, means simply 'reflection of the moon'.

Ying Yue is almost ... but not quite.
Ying Yue is very nearly ... but not actually.

Aw. Never mind.

What people don't realise about Ying Yue is that she is invisible (to all intents and purposes). Nobody ever really notices her. Even that 'special' teacher at school – who you always see featured prominently in heartfelt documentaries about the gradual decline of the British educational system – even that special teacher never bothered to notice Ying Yue.

Ying Yue believes she may actually become *altogether invisible* whenever she holds her breath.

Nobody has ever indicated otherwise.

Ying Yue cannot speak Chinese. But she *can* understand it. Bits of it, at least. Although nothing ever really sticks with Ying Yue. She is ferociously innocent. She is so innocent that sometimes she forgets that she is a person and believes, instead, that she is a small, insignificant white feather – a little piece of fluff – drifting gently – in an infinitely descending circle – down,

down,

down, to the ground.

Does that make any sense? If something is infinitely descending can it ever actually reach the ground?

Wouldn't the ground – its presence, its absence – be immaterial?

Ying Yue's not sure that even Wang Shu knows that her only daughter can't speak Chinese. Nobody on earth is more Chinese than Wang Shu, or more proud of being Chinese than Wang Shu. Every follicle and mole and pore on Wang Shu's body is Chinese. Wang Shu sweats green tea.

Or maybe Wang Shu *does* know. Maybe Wang Shu *does* know that her only daughter doesn't speak Chinese. Maybe Wang Shu never actually *wanted* Ying Yue to learn. To maintain a sense of distance.

What an extraordinarily interesting and yet strangely complicated/disturbing thought that is.

Fei Hung – Ying Yue's wonderful younger brother (Ying Yue was just a failed try-out for a boy) – *can* speak Chinese. Fei Hung is the Golden Child. Everything about Fei Hung is perfect. Fei Hung actually means 'bright future'. Fei Hung actually means 'a swan-goose soaring high in the sky'.

Although ...

Argh. Forget it.

Charles must be fifty-odd years old, Avigail sur-mises (Charles is actually forty years old). Charles makes beautiful bespoke teddy bears for a living. Avigail still can't entirely come to terms with this notion. It seems like such a silly and improbable way to spend your time. Pointless. Facile. And Charles ... There is nothing cute or quaint about Charles. He is uncomfortably tall and pale and his dark hair is long and centre-parted. It hangs in straight flaps either side of his face. And the T-shirts! Avigail doesn't think for a second that Charles is really a fan of Alanis Morissette, but during her last visit he was wearing a shirt that read: *It's like 10,000 knives when all you need is a spoon.*

Malc (the prospective buyer) had benignly refer-enced the T-shirt when they were first introduced and it had instantly set off some kind of neurotic response in Charles. He had promptly let slip about the burglary. And the knife (did he do it all on purpose? Had he planned it? Was he actually a self-sabotager? One of those self-sabotagers who doesn't even know – who isn't even *aware* – that they are self-sabotaging? Avigail has bumped up against her fair share of self-sabotagers in her life and is certainly in no hurry to make the acquaintance of another).

Nobody has even mentioned the T-shirt this time around, though (since Charles isn't wearing it, and since they have literally only just stepped in through the front door), yet Charles has still felt compelled to mention the burglary. *Already!* Avigail suspects that Charles will always mention the burglary from now on during viewings. Out of sheer habit.

He's such a fuck-up.

Charles is a kind of Frankenstein. Well, no. What Avigail actually means is that he's a kind of Frankenstein's monster. He reminds Avigail of the Native American character in the film of *One Flew Over the Cuckoo's Nest*. What was that guy's name? Chief ...?

Chief ...?
Gets smothered by a pillow in the end.
Very sad. Although it's actually a blessing. Because he has no quality of life. Um. Or was it Jack Nicholson's

character – McMurphy – who is smothered by Chief?

Yes.

Avigail briefly imagines smothering Charles with a pillow.

Hmm. It *would* actually be a blessing. Because he *doesn't* really have any quality of life.

Surrounded by all this *stuff*.

There's a flatness to Charles. An otherworldliness. A deathly pallor.

Charles has a sewing room which is full of multi-coloured samples of mohair and buttons and kapok for stuffing. He doesn't like talking about the bears because he isn't particularly interested in the bears so he doesn't bother. There is no profound emotional/spiritual connection to the bears – at least, none that he is aware of. But he is emotionally illiterate so he can't be 100 per cent sure. Although he is 75 per cent sure.

Charles just got into making the bears as a sideline to gratify a woman he enjoyed a brief relationship with who ran a toy shop in the picturesque but puffed-up Cinque Port town of Rye. He had once worked, briefly, while still a student (he studied architecture – dropped out in his final year), as an industrial machinist.
He acquired skills.

Then the whole 'bear thing' just took off. Almost by accident. Almost 'in spite of'.
Charles really is surprisingly good at making bears.

Although of late he has taken to making the bears but feeling unable to part with them once they are completed. Even if they have been commissioned.
Yes. Even bears with a sad and touching personal history connecting them, inviolably, to the person who has commissioned them. Heirloom bears. Post-bereavement bears. Totemic bears who represent something – or someone – tragically lost. Bears – for example – wearing a dress or a suit fashioned out of a former loved-one's favourite garment or with a tiny pocket containing the ashes (in a special, sparkly-red vial placed in the approximate location of the heart area) of a lost parent or child or pet or lover.

Avigail notices that Charles has rather beautiful, delicate hands. Long fingers. Neat nails. And he never smells bad. He is clean. Which is some, slight, compensation, she supposes.

She knows that OCD and hoarding are related conditions so his rigorous personal hygiene makes a weird kind of sense to her.

Yes, that much, at least, she understands.

People really *do* bore Avigail half to death. She much prefers buildings. Buildings are just like people but they stay in one place and are generally open and hospitable. And they talk, but only very, very quietly. In hushed tones.

Avigail was raised in a Hasidic Jewish community. She didn't prosper there. Her spirit rebelled against it. She wouldn't conform. Her 'out' was anorexia. Long spells in hospital, months in special units, distant referrals, gradually – stealthily – establishing contacts and relationships in the REAL WORLD outside the Hasidic community. Just subtly, just tentatively. Over time.

A painstaking adaptation.

Avigail – like Wang Shu – is a die-hard pragmatist.

Fucking dreamers and idealists can all go hang.

Avigail fought tooth and nail to be here. *Here*. In this God-awful shithole, with these idiotic fucking morons. **RIGHT NOW**.

'She didn't actually break in,' Avigail reiterates.

Avigail is irritated with Charles for mentioning the burglary, twice.

Charles is looking at Avigail with a frown.

She?!

Why would Avigail possibly imagine that the potential thief could've been female?

And why is she called A-vi-gail instead of A-bi-gail?

'Perhaps *she* got disturbed,' he mutters. Slight roll of the eyes.

Avigail really has some nerve trying to appropriate his burglary narrative like that.

She?

Seriously?
She?!
In therapeutic circles that would be called ... uh ...
What would they call that?

'Perhaps a seagull?' Ying Yue murmurs these words quietly while gazing down, self-effacingly, at the scuffed, tiled floor. Then she removes her hand from the lovely, brown saddle – which has been worn deliciously smooth by the endless friction of Charles's dead mother's thighs – and performs a little – and quite funny – mime of something crashing into her head.
'Perhaps disturbed by a seagull?' she reiterates with a husky laugh. 'The burglar?'
  Already Ying Yue feels like her volume button has been turned down to virtually inaudible.

Who turned the button down?
She glances around her, blinking.

Did Ying Yue turn the button down?
(Ying Yue often refers to herself in the third person.)

She blinks, then smiles.

23

Oh, look!
Ying Yue is a tiny pinch of sand!
On a giant, sandy beach!

Let's build sandcastles!

They are all still standing by the front door. It feels like they have been standing there, huddled together, in a pack, for ever.

'Sorry? Did … is that a mime of … did you just mime a seagull shitting on your head, Ying Yue?' Avigail finally pipes up, confused.
Ying Yue has a way of talking – a way of looking down and swallowing her words – that makes it hard to follow what she says.
'I apologise for using the word "shit",' Avigail adds, as an afterthought (although, even in so doing, she uses it for a second time).
'Shit. Yes. *No!* Shit! Heaven forbid!' Charles echoes, drolly.

He immediately imagines a T-shirt that reads: *I sincerely apologise for using the word*

SHHHI
IIIIIIIT
TTT!

Charles patently still has some growing up to do.

As she speaks, Avigail is inspecting Ying Yue's head. Ying Yue's head seems fine. Although her hair is slightly greasy. Ying Yue points – with a clumsy, submissive gesture – towards Wang Shu.

'Oh. Okay. Did a seagull ...?'
Ying Yue draws breath. 'An oyster shell. It fell down from the sky. *Psssseeeeeuuuuuu!* Dropped by a bird. It clipped Wang Shu's head. There is some blood.

A little blood. But Wang Shu is fine. Wang Shu is good.'

'Seriously?' Avigail scratches her own head. 'This was ... You mean outside? Just this minute? An *oyster* shell? Over on Trevor Street? But why didn't I ... why didn't you just *say* something?'

Avigail is confused. She has no memory of this incident – this curious little drama. She replays the walk up Trevor Street with Wang Shu and Ying Yue in her mind but can't recall anything remotely untoward ...

Nope. Nothing.

Just the normal sales pitch about the local area – not that this was remotely necessary, since Wang Shu and Ying Yue both work, full-time, on Llandudno pier (Ying Yue collects the tokens on the Bouncy Castle) and they know the town extremely well.

Although ... uh ... Didn't Avigail just think some negative gull thoughts – literally moments ago? Perhaps she was aware – at a subconscious level – of something untoward having recently occurred?

And wasn't there a phone call? On her mobile? Didn't she receive a phone call from the office just as . . .?

Nah. This makes no sense.
Avigail demands that the world make sense. At least *her* tiny piece of it – the tiny bit that she so carefully and rigorously marshals.

Charles winces. He holds the popcorn maker even closer to his chest as if to protect it from the horror of random accidents.

Don't worry, popcorn maker. You'll be fine. Never fear. *I'll* look after you, I promise.

x

'It's okay,' Ying Yue explains, 'Ma dabbed the blood off with this tissue.'

Dabbed!

What a funny word! Ying Yue thinks, and smiles at her capacity to astonish herself.

Avigail sees that (a now mysteriously smiling) Ying Yue is clutching a bloody tissue in the hand of her good arm. Wang Shu is still talking, animatedly, in a harsh, rasping voice, on the phone, apparently completely unperturbed by what has happened.

Avigail peers into Wang Shu's short, chaotic, clumsily cropped head of hair and detects a kind of dampness – a reddish-blackness – down one side, just behind the right ear. She also sees a patch of something suspiciously like blood on Wang Shu's shoulder.

'Ma is very strong.' Ying Yue bows, proudly. 'Nothing worries her. She is very tough. A tough lady. Like ... uh ...' she muses for a second, '... water off a duck's back.'

She beams.

Charles looks over at Avigail, disquieted. Avigail is an estate agent who has been hired by the bank. The bank have had a gutful of Charles but are trying to play ball because it still suits them to do so. Although they really don't give a damn about Charles – or any of their stupid customers. The TV adverts to the opposite effect are all just a hoax, a dreadful lie.

Avigail is dressed somewhat inappropriately for her role, which Charles finds confusing. Avigail dresses as though she might be going out for cocktails. Avigail dresses for another, better kind of life. Her skirt is trimmed with sequins.

'Are you going out for cocktails?' Charles suddenly wonders, apropos of nothing.
'Pardon?'
Avigail glances down at herself.
'Are you …?' Charles starts to repeat himself and then stops and swallows, realising what an idiot he sounds.

Cocktails?!

Must. Think. Before. Speak.

'Cocktails? Seriously, Charles?' Avigail snorts. 'In Llandudno? On a Wednesday afternoon?'
Charles just laughs, nervously.

'No. *No!* Cocktails?! Why would you even *say* that?' she persists.

Avigail regrets having used Charles's name a few moments before. There was a slight atmosphere of condescension – of judgement – in it, she knows. And then 'Why would you even *say* that?' suddenly sounds – just the tone, the delivery – very Jewish, very Jewish mother-y. Good gracious!

But why *would* he say that?! Intonation aside?

Cocktails?!

And why *now*? In the middle of this whole combustible seagull situation which may well prove catastrophic to the potential sale?

Charles bites his lip and his Toxic Super-Ego hisses, '*You fucking* **idiot**. *Now she'll despise you. And who can really blame her if she does?*'

In truth, Charles doesn't especially care what Avigail thinks of him, but he does care how her potentially despising him might (indeed, does) make him feel about himself. If that makes any kind of sense. Hmm. He scowls. *Does* that actually make any kind of sense?

It's not that he's incredibly self-involved …

(*Am* I just incredibly self-involved?)

... it's simply that he has no remaining illusions about how the world sees him. How it feels about him. How it despises him. The whole world. How it judges him. Finds him ridiculous. Finds him inadequate. Finds him wanting. Always.
That's all.
But hey ...

FUCK *YOU*, YEAH?
AND *FUCK* YOUR STUPID WORLD!

This is a perfect example of Trauma Tunnel Embitterment. Charles knows, in his heart, that there's nothing really wrong with the world. There's only a problem with how he – post trauma – *views* the world. This is why he needs to get started on the course.

But he can't get started.

Richard Grannon has clearly outlined in the module on Mental Toughness ('Let's *get shit done!*') that people with Charles's instinctive psychological 'response' (e.g. Emotional Flashbacks/Bloated Super-Ego/Trauma Tunnel Embitterment) often find it difficult to embrace change, to initiate new modes of behaviour, to – deep inhale – *just get started*. For this very reason Richard Grannon has included a handy sixteen-minute hypnosis session in one of the appendices that gently talks the *Silencing the Inner Critic* member through the special blocks and nega-tive thought patterns that may stop them from getting properly under way with the course.

But a person – a member – would naturally need to get under way with the course before they might hope to locate and subsequently employ this helpful strategy.

Grannon discusses this paradox – with great passion and alacrity – in the live webcasts that accompany the course, two of which Charles has watched – with close attention – while hoovering.

Charles knows that he exaggerates how bad his dad was. His dad never called him a 'pathetic piece of crap' but the message was there, in looks and gestures and a chronic want of eye contact – or a chronic excess of eye contact. Which was it?

Neither?
Both?

In truth he can't be bothered thinking about all this stuff. He's scared of it. And he's bored of it. And Grannon doesn't believe there's any point in trawling through old memories to work out why everything's fucked up. It takes too long. And it'd be confusing. Although it depends where you are on the Cognitive Post Traumatic Stress Response scale (yes, a 'Response' – they don't call it a 'Disorder' any more because Grannon believes these behaviours *can* be unlearned). If you are over 5 on the CPTSR scale (the scale runs 1–10) then you should probably also be seeking therapeutic support in conjunction with the course. Charles hasn't entirely processed this idea yet.

He isn't sure where he is on the scale. He hasn't got around to working it out.

There are four basic responses to trauma: fight, flight, freeze, fawn.
Charles runs from life/conflict (flight) and freezes under stress (retreats into his imagination).

Oh. And he over-intellectualises instead of simply feeling.

He certainly isn't warlike (fight).
And he isn't really a people person (fawn).
He only very rarely offers compliments.
Hardly ever.
Never.

It's just a question of calmly and systematically re-patterning the way that you think. It shouldn't take long – a couple of months, at most. In fact some people have reported feeling a giant weight lifting from their shoulders after only two or three days. The material is so effective. It's revolutionary. But as soon as Grannon uttered the dread words 'after only two or three days' Charles knew that he was now set up to fail. Because there was no way he would ever feel better that quickly. He is too damaged. And he is hyper-competitive. And he is a sore loser. And even if he *did* feel better that quickly then he probably wouldn't actually realise because he can never really tell how he feels because he is emotionally illiterate, and automatically over-intellectualises or disappears into fantasy when things get too challenging.

Charles's father is a recently retired fisherman in Conwy. Charles's father fished for plaice, mullet, whiting, codling and dab off Conwy for over forty years. Charles's father had a brief affair with Charles's mother (Branimira) but then chose to stay with his wife of seventeen years. Charles's three older half-brothers still crew Charles's father's boat. Mainly they use it to take tourists out on jaunts and to ferry the wind-farm workers back and forth. The boat is called *TRI BRAWD*, which is Welsh for *THREE BROTHERS*.

Fuck fuck fuck fuck fuck.

Richard Grannon has emphasised that it is important – nay, vital – to find a vocabulary with which to describe how you are feeling.
Words are the harbingers of feelings.

Fuck fuck fuck fuck fuck.

Even if you *aren't* feeling. That's okay, too. You just need to check in, every day, and ask yourself a couple of simple questions about how things are going.
Jot down some notes in a pad.

Charles immediately paused the recording and went online and spent several hours trying to find the perfect pad to jot down notes in. He ended up buying five pads with nice, hard covers in a special Amazon Prime deal. They were a good price but they were unlined. After he had placed the order he realised, to his horror, that he doesn't actually *like* unlined pages. They seem …

Hmm. The word?

Engulfing.

Like a black hole.
But just all … all … all *white*.
A *white* hole.

AAaaaaaaaaahhhhhhhh!!!!!!!

TRI BRAWD.

Fuck fuck fuck fuck fuck.

How am I feeling? Charles wonders.

I am feeling ...

Claustrophobic.
Disgusted.
Nervous.
Stupid.
Fastidious.
Sad.

Alone.

Charles worries that he may have shingles.

'Would you mind showing Ying Yue and Wang Shu through to the kitchen while I pop outside for a minute, Charles?' Avigail asks, as Charles scratches gingerly at a suspicious rash on his upper forearm. 'Perhaps you might ... I don't know ... bathe her head in some warm, salted water? I just need to pop outside for a second – I won't be ... uh ... long ... if that's okay ...?'

Avigail promptly disappears, leaving a delectable cloud of Body Shop Japanese Cherry Blossom Strawberry Kiss Eau de Toilette in her wake.

Wang Shu is still on the phone, talking in Chinese.

'Bathe her *head*?' Charles murmurs, horrified.
'There's no need,' Ying Yue pipes up. 'Mother is tough. She hates any fuss. She doesn't welcome any fuss.'
After she finishes speaking Ying Yue quietly inspects all the locks on Charles's front door.
'Plenty locks,' she says, approvingly.

Ferocious innocence.
No judgement.
Nothing.

'Ha. Yes …' Charles almost winces (making up for Ying Yue's lack of judgement by sternly judging himself). 'To keep me in!'
Ying Yue glances up, thoughtfully, and still, miraculously, no sign of judgement.
'Uh … joke …' Charles mutters.
'Ah.' Ying Yue smiles broadly.

Ying Yue doesn't really understand jokes. And she doesn't really speak English. I mean … she isn't … she can't … not … not *really*. She doesn't truly speak *any* language. Well, she *can* speak, just a smattering, but she doesn't fully *possess* any language. And no language fully possesses her. She slips and trips and falls cheerfully between the letters. Yes. That's her. That's Ying Yue, holding on for dear life to the lip of an e, the tail of a q.

It's quite impermanent, quite temporary – her grasp of these things. Everything's just hashed together, just piecemeal, just loosely tacked into some semblance of coherence – of intelligibility – by giant, scruffy stitches of sincerity, simplicity and goodwill.

Charles suddenly crosses himself, in his mind, for protection, even though he isn't currently – never has been, and never will be – a Catholic.

Protection from what, exactly, he doesn't yet know. Perhaps he never will.

2.

EVERY TIME YOU MAKE A TYPO, THE ERRORISTS WIN

Perfectionism is actually a major part of the problem. Perfectionism and entitlement.

Charles knows this. He understands that his fervent desire for things to be 'just so' is a stupidly *anal*, self-involved, un-evolved way of being. Grannon sometimes links 'entitled' behaviour (a modern scourge) to a tendency that is found to be prevalent in the Cluster B Personality Disorder Matrix called 'Magical Thinking'. This is something that very small children with porous ego-boundaries are apt to engage in, i.e. believing that their internal urges/desires will somehow be 'magically' expressed in the outside word.

The Toxic Inner Critic is behind this craving for perfection, surely? The Parent voice? The hectoring voice? The 'moral' voice?

Never satisfied. Always looking for a weakness. Always sniffing out a problem, an inconsistency, a dreadful flaw.

Richard Grannon's mantra is 'Good enough is *more* than enough for me.' He came up with this idea of good-enoughness as a teenager – imagine that! A *teenager* – while he was living in Portugal among wolves – being raised by wolves. Then one day the Alpha wolf – the pack leader, an amazingly accepting, generous, infinitely wise wolf called Ranwa – was struck by lightning and died and Grannon had to step up to the mark and fight his beloved wolf brother, Simco, for the head role. Simco was a good and kind wolf but he was weak. He was indecisive. So Grannon honestly had no option but to challenge him for dominance. For the well-being – nay, survival – of the entire wolf community.

Uh-oh.
Do you see that?
Do you see how the Toxic Inner Critic is trying to belittle Grannon with a blitzkrieg of blithe sarcasm?

Ha ha *ha*.

Grannon wasn't raised by wolves. Although from what Charles can deduce Grannon spent part of his childhood in a Portuguese commune, which isn't really that different, is it? A commune in Portugal?

Oh, it's all so *enviably* cosmopolitan.

Charles suspects that Richard Grannon speaks about five different languages. He imagines that Grannon has a 'smattering' of German and passable Thai and that he would positively *thrive* in Brazil.
Richard Grannon speaks his excellent English with a broad Scouse accent (more marked when he's feeling especially ebullient or pissed or tired).
Richard Grannon adheres to the fight/fawn archetype.

Charles has made quite a study of this by watching all his posts on YouTube.

(That's quite a lot of posts.)

Grannon teaches that you should closely study the people you admire and try to actively impersonate the good qualities you find in them. This is an NLP strategy.

Grannon isn't just a therapist, remember? He's a life coach.

He is receptive.
He is flexible.
He is open to change.

Avigail doesn't actually lock the door behind her (there are too many locks – Charles is a freak) but leaves it on the latch (even though she has a spare set of keys) and quickly turns left down Ty Isa Road, heading back towards Trevor Street. Avigail really loves Trevor Street despite its unbearable, seasonal gull problem. It's very close to the seafront and the houses on one side are pebbledash cottages, all set back behind low, stone walls with nice, manageable gardens. On the other side are the traditional, seaside terraces: two-storey but with sweet, little pitched windows in every roof. There's a polite, artisan vibe on the left, offset by a more traditional, seaside feel on the right. Nothing too arty-farty.

Cocktails?!
Charles is a pest.
A *pest*.

Avigail reaches the near end of Trevor Street and stands there, firmly planting her feet, sternly squinting up it.

Gull-shit-splattered everywhere – like a real-time Jackson Pollock.

Oyster shell … Oyster shell …

?

She walks slowly up the road scanning the tarmac and the pavement. It isn't a long road. She looks for the oyster shell. Nothing. No sign of an oyster shell. Where is the oyster shell?

Avigail closes her eyes for a moment and tries to recall exactly what happened on her earlier journey up Trevor Street.
She plays an edited version in her mind.

Nope. Nothing.

It couldn't be considered 'normal', surely, to be so oblivious? So unaware? So absent? So absent that an oyster shell can fall from the sky and hit a client on the head? For an oyster shell to fall from the sky and hit a client on the head and draw blood?

Do I trust them? Avigail wonders, slightly paranoid.

Wang Shu and Ying Yue?
Are they trustworthy?

Is this a prank?

A joke?

A set-up?

Avigail needs to be perfectly normal. She needs to be the most normal, most present, most effortlessly functional person in *every* situation, in *every* environment.
Avigail *longs* to conform to the wider culture ABSOLUTELY.

Even though she is secretly at war with the algorithm. Even though she secretly calls other human beings 'fleshies'.

Even though she secretly makes abstract tapestries which attempt to depict the *ruah hakodesh*.
Even though she secretly thinks the Reverend Thomas Robert Malthus gets a bad rap.
Even though she makes her own foundation by combining three different foundations and a fragrance-free hand cream.
Even though she sometimes wears sequins during daylight hours.

Why do I always get found out?!
For the smallest, the most insignificant of breaches, dammit?!

A car sounds its horn in the distance.

Avigail opens her eyes and sees a car driving up the promenade, and beyond that, beyond the mew of gulls, the roar of the sea, beyond all these – beyond the honking car – she suddenly

CHING!

feels *the spaces between things.*

Space *as* substance.

A slight shift in perception.

Like the feeling of disorientation when you are just about to swoon ...

Something <small>utterly insignificant</small> greatly magnified and rendered dreadfully significant.

Oh no, no, no.
Avigail shakes her head.
Oh no, no, no.
Not here! Not now!

Don't let this happen again!

The quiet *in* sound – the energy *in* space. The movement *in* stillness which is the hallmark of ...

of ...

Don't utter it!
Don't *name* it!
Don't give it the opportunity ... the elbow-room!

Avigail will not be appropriated.

No.

She will resist!
She will stand her ground!

She refuses to be hijacked!
Here!
Now!
At approximately 2.45 p.m. on Trevor Street in Llandudno by ... by ... by ...

Argh!

NO!

The
Transcendent
One!

Duh, duh, *DUUUUH*!

The oyster shell! A hoax! A simple ruse! To bring her out here so she might be devoured, be consumed by *Ein Sof*!

A helpless offering.
A rebellious *hors d'oeuvre*.

Avigail tries to turn but cannot turn. The something-in-nothing, solid-in-space, quiet-in-sound energy – the awareness – the tiny adjustment – the *shift* – is consuming everything, entering everything, transforming everything but leaving all things *exactly the same*. Ah, such omnipresence, such savage-quiet-gentleness, such irreducible implacability …

Immanence.

All God.

All complete.

Everywhere.
In everything.

Leit Atar panuy mi-neya, as her father was often wont
to say.

(No site is devoid of it.)

Ein Sof.

The Unending.

'I starved you out, damn you!' Avigail groans, then
– using every inch of her remaining power – she
hurls herself over a low garden wall and crouches
there.

Hiding.
Hiding from *Ein Sof.*

Which is impossible. And ridiculous. But she's been doing it her entire life.
Because *Ein Sof* allows free will.
That's the whole point.
Isn't it?

Time – obligingly – passes (and also – quite unhelp-fully – stands still).

'Avigail ...? Um. Hello? Avigail?'

It is Charles. He has followed Avigail down the road.

Please don't let that be Charles, Avigail thinks.
Although who else could it possibly be?
She opens her eyes. It is Charles.

Charles has been illumined by *Ein Sof* but doesn't yet seem to realise (the idiot).
Have *I* been illumined? Avigail wonders. She peers down at herself.
She can't really tell.

Perhaps she is in denial?

Screw 'denial'! She has no time for 'denial'.
Avigail is a great grasper of nettles.
She *likes* the sting!

Is the garden wall illumined?
Yes. The wall seems illumined. Everything is illumined.

Everything *is* illumined.

'Are you feeling okay, Charles?' Avigail asks from her crouching position (opting to take the initiative).
'I ...' Charles is about to ask Avigail why she is hiding behind a wall and then is saved from this awkward necessity by a woman coming out of the house and asking Avigail what she is doing crouching in her flowerbed.

The woman is illumined.

'Oh, hi.' Avigail rises to her feet. 'I am searching for evidence,' she announces, with a slight air of foreboding.
'Evidence?'

The garden is illumined.

'A client of mine was injured by an oyster shell which was dropped by a seagull and I am looking for that oyster shell. As evidence. She has a head wound. It's quite serious, actually.'
The woman silently processes this information.

The cottage is illumined.

'If you happen to see a bloodied oyster shell – here, in the local vicinity – I'd be incredibly grateful if you could contact me.'
Avigail hunts around in her handbag and pulls out a business card.
'Here's my card.' She points. 'My name is Avigail. A-*vi*-gail. These are my contact details: mobile, email…'
She strides towards the woman and hands her the card. The woman takes the card.

The business card is illumined.

Am *I* illumined? Avigail wonders.

Damn you! Damn you, Ein Sof!

The illumined woman thanks Avigail for the illumined business card.

'Thank *you*,' Avigail responds. 'And sorry for the ... you know ... disturbance.'

She takes the woman's hand and shakes it, ceremoniously.

Yes. Extremely cordial. Utterly measured. Very calm. Perfectly normal.

She then strides back towards Charles. Out through the gate this time. She clicks the latch shut with a distinct touch of brio.

The latch is illumined. *Click-ick-ick-ick.* It *sings*.

'Are you all right, there, Charles?' she asks again. 'Where are Ying Yue and Wang Shu?'
'I came to fetch you because I didn't feel comfortable showing them around on my own,' Charles says limply.

Charles is illumined. But he's still Charles.
Alas.

'Do you feel different?' Avigail wonders, inspecting Charles's illumined face.

'Sorry?'

'Like soft water. You know how it is when water is hard – it's been heavily processed, is full of chemicals – but then it's filtered and it becomes kind of … softer … chalky?'

Charles gazes at Avigail for a few seconds and then says slowly, 'I'm not sure if I'm really capable of answering that question, Avigail.'

'Not to worry.' Avigail shrugs. 'I just wondered.'

'I didn't want to leave the door on the latch,' Charles explains. 'You have some … uh … soil on your skirt.'

Charles doesn't want to admit that he has suddenly become nervous around Ying Yue. There's a kind of …

What is it?
Impossible to say.

Something new.
Something distinctly alien.

'It's twelve years since the attempted burglary.' Avigail dusts the mud off as she walks. 'Last year there were six burglaries in Llandudno, which totals at 2.6 per cent of all crime in the town. Burglary is not a serious problem in Llandudno. It's only a problem in Llandudno if you *choose* to make it a problem.'

'There's a small issue with the bailiff,' Charles explains, ignoring this.

As they walk up the road and approach Charles's house they stroll past a tiny, elderly man who is wearing a giant pair of dark glasses and holding a white cane. He is standing next to a large, blue, waste disposal bin. He is perfectly still.

The blind old man is illumined.

'I see. Yes. Isn't that your cat?' Avigail points.

A hairless Sphynx cat is mooching down the road. It is Morpheus. Charles curses and trots after Morpheus.

Morpheus is illumined.

Morpheus makes no attempt to avoid Charles on his approach. He is passive. Charles picks him up.

Illumined man. Illumined cat.

'I pulled the door shut behind me,' he grumbles. 'I've no idea how he got out.'

'Let's get inside,' Avigail suggests (determined to snap out of her stupid, trippy head-space), 'and try to salvage what remains of this viewing, shall we?'

Charles follows Avigail back into the house. He senses that Avigail thinks *he* is the problem when in actual fact *she* is the problem. Yes. Avigail seems to be exhibiting a mode of behaviour which Grannon may well call 'blame shifting'.

Avigail's 'Reality Filter' is all fucked up, Charles thinks.

Seriously.

She's nuts.
Crouching behind the wall like that?!

He puts Morpheus down and shuts the door.

Hmm. He shoots a bolt, thoughtfully.

The 'somatic' body? What *is* 'the somatic body'? What did Grannon *mean* by 'the somatic body'?

Must Google.

They find Wang Shu and Ying Yue in the kitchen. Wang Shu is on the phone talking in Chinese. Ying Yue is poking an inquisitive finger through a small hole in a pair of Charles's Y-fronts which are hung on a large, rectangular drying rack.

She seems to be holding her breath. Or if she isn't, she exhales, sharply (for no discernible reason), when Charles and Avigail enter the room.

Charles ignores Ying Yue. Ying Yue is freaking him out. Instead he glances over at Avigail and wonders if there is anything about her – anything at all – that might be worth emulating. Avigail must be all of twenty-five years old (Avigail is actually thirty-five years old) and has a funny way of tensing her right cheek and glaring intently at a person when she's concentrating. It's a kind of grimace – almost a tic. Her dedication to her work – her … passion? Drive? Focus? Diligence? It's certainly notable – interesting – almost admirable. But no. No. That's not something Charles would want to impersonate. He fleetingly wonders whether Avigail is a perfectionist. And whether Avigail herself has any role models; people she aspires to emulate?

There *is* actually someone.

Avigail aspires to be like Lucy Molloy, the Perth-based YouTube housewife/tattoo model.

Given a thousand guesses, Charles would never have imagined Lucy Molloy was Avigail's role model. This is mainly because Charles has no idea who Lucy Molloy is. And he doesn't know Avigail very well. But there are other reasons, too.

Ying Yue knows, though!
Ying Yue knows who Lucy Molloy is!
Ying Yue *also* worships at the altar of Lucy Molloy! This is a powerful tie – a profound connection – between Ying Yue and Avigail, but unfortunately neither of them is aware of it or is likely to find out about it, either, during this brief, twenty-minute house viewing.

Such a shame.

Good enough is *more* than enough for me!

That's the mantra. That's the phrase that Grannon came up with as a perfectionist teen.

Good enough is *more* than enough. For me.

They are in the kitchen. The short entrance hall leads straight into a dark, poky kitchen. There is some rather astonishing 1970s tilework in here by the famous designer Alan Wallwork, although much of it is obscured by a random collection of stuff (some still unopened and in its original packaging) which litters the counters.

It has never struck Charles as remotely 'ironic' that a celebrated designer of tiles should be called 'Wallwork'. Given Charles's advanced grasp of this particular comic form/rhetorical device, such an oversight on his part could probably be seen *as* 'ironic'.

Ah, but 'the world is incorrigibly plural … crazier and more of it than we think', as the great poet· Louis MacNeice was oft wont to say (although not quite in that order).

These tiles are definitely an acquired taste. Charles doesn't like the tiles but he is very, very attached to them for some inexplicable reason probably connected to his mother, Branimira. And, as luck would have it, Charles has recently taken the opportunity to do a load of washing. About five ironic T-shirts – one of which reads: *Every time you make a typo, the errorists win* – some baggy, black Y-fronts and some black socks are hung over the heated bars of a free-standing electric clothes dryer. A rack.

The room is consequently very hot.

Wang Shu is still talking on the phone in Chinese.

On the very rare occasions when Wang Shu isn't talking on the phone in Chinese she enjoys watching YouTube footage of cats falling.

Someone or something scaring the shit out of a cat makes her laugh so hard and so loud that sometimes her loving daughter Ying Yue fears for her well-being. And her sanity. She laughs and laughs and laughs until she sobs. And then suddenly – in an instant – every inch of happiness is sucked – by a giant, black vortex – out of the world and Wang Shu is rendered inconsolable.

This has made Ying Yue suspicious of pleasure. Ying Yue has not been raised in a faith tradition but she senses that pleasure often has dire consequences. The Christians were completely right about that.

'Do you have a bin, Charles?' Avigail asks.
Avigail could happily punch Charles square in the face for opting to do his washing today and for hanging it on a sodding free-standing heated rack in the tiny kitchen and then loitering next to it, hugely, and draining all available light and air from the room.

Avigail's mother actually used a rather more antique version of this particular kind of dryer when she was a girl. It brings back bittersweet memories for Avigail. Whenever Avigail was home from hospital as a teen she would sit in the kitchen, gazing at her plate of gefilte fish patties (she was a slow eater until she stopped eating altogether) and imagine that the dryer was some kind of Tardis. A time machine that she could climb inside and use to travel to distant epochs/different galaxies. Yes. Away.

AWAY FROM FAMILY.

AWAY FROM GOD.

Charles has neglected to cover the rack in a sheet or duvet cover. Avigail believes that this is key. The idea is to do your sheets and duvets – your household linens – in the first wash so that when you do your personal items – your vests, smalls etc. in the second wash they can be hung within a modest curtain of fabric, the warm air is contained, and the dryer is therefore rendered both more cost-effective and more productive.

Charles is standing next to his kitchen bin with his foot applied to the little pedal so the lid is standing proud.

'Would you like to dispose of your tissue in Charles's kitchen bin, Ying Yue?' Avigail asks, pointing.

Ying Yue is still clutching the bloodied tissue. She looks over towards the bin. She frowns and focuses very hard. Then she screws the tissue up into a tight ball and lobs it towards the bin. The overall distance between Ying Yue and the bin is about three feet, in total. There is no discernible reason for Ying Yue not to step forward and gently place the tissue into the bin. But she throws the tissue. And she misses the bin. The tissue hits Charles in the groin area and then ricochets on to the kitchen lino and slides across the floor. Before anyone can move to retrieve it, Morpheus, who has been loitering around in the hallway, darts into the kitchen to attack the tissue and play pitter-pat with it between his funny, naked, pink paws. Because Wang Shu has been talking on the phone (in Chinese) all the while, she has only been partially aware of the transaction re the tissue and is completely unaware of the existence of Morpheus. When Morpheus suddenly darts into the kitchen, Wang Shu (who is still talking on the phone) takes him – in his hairless state – to be some kind of bizarrely distended rat. A terrifying, supernatural creature. She screams (of course Wang Shu does not scream – she is constitutionally incapable of anything as feminine and pointless as screaming – she yells, she squawks, like an irate raven) and springs away from Morpheus into the gap between the fridge/freezer and the door. Unfortunately any sudden movement in a room so full of stuff is liable to cause a measure of disruption. Wang Shu knocks into the fridge/freezer on top of which Charles stores not only his kettle, but a tea tray full of tea accoutrements, and a second

65

and a third kettle (which he has reason to believe will be more ergonomic/faster/cheaper to boil/less prone to producing limescale etc. than the one he currently uses), plus a collection of black teas, white teas, green teas and smoked teas, and teas to aid the promotion of digestion, sleep, liver and kidney regulation, nasal decongestion, calm, serenity etc. etc.

Avigail moves (her lightning responses are something Charles *does* find enviable) to support Wang Shu, although she finds herself actually unable to *touch* Wang Shu in the final instant because Wang Shu seems to have an inviolable space around her which it is absolutely impossible to penetrate (this is an essential part of something which – in informal lingo – you might call Wang Shu's 'personality'), so Avigail diverts to catch a couple of the items currently falling from on top of the fridge/freezer (a tea for menstrual cramps, a silver-plated cream jug).

Ying Yue (as Wang Shu's mirror) is compelled to mimic her mother's reaction (but with a little more finesse) so also springs back, in shock, against the surface behind her and accidentally knocks into a broom that happens to be leaning there. The broom falls forward. The broom's handle knocks into Avigail (first), then hits the very tip of Wang

Shu's trainer (after). Wang Shu yells again – even louder (if that's remotely possible) – and drops her phone.

Wang Shu's sacred phone!
Where is Wang Shu without her phone?!
Who is Wang Shu without her phone?

Can this really be happening?!

As she catches the jug Avigail has a sudden – unconnected – thought. She thinks.
Oh. *I see* ... Everything *is* illumined. Of course. Everything is illumined –

speciality tea, cream jug ...

Everything is illumined. Always. Constantly. Perpetually. Ineffably. Illumined. All of matter. Illumined. It's just a question of quietly glancing down, focusing ...

Ein Sof, in everything, NOW.
Ein Sof is always in the present tense.
Ein Sof never was. *Ein Sof* IS.

The broom clatters to the ground. The broom is illumined. Ying Yue makes no attempt to grab the broom because being hit by a broom (even an illumined broom) is considered *INCREDIBLY BAD LUCK* to the Chinese. Charles – who has very slow reflexes – does nothing. Morpheus is thoroughly traumatised by everything (the squawking, the sudden movements, the phone, the illumined broom) and piles straight into the illumined drying rack. The rack teeter-totters (Charles – finally spurred into action – stills it with a single, calm movement of the hand) and Morpheus performs a quick 180-degree turn, exiting the rack (head and torso obliterated by a T-shirt that reads: *I support the right to arm bears*).

Because Morpheus is unable to see where he is going, but is terrified, he (illumined cat) careers straight into the fallen (illumined) broom, panics still further, continues his forward momentum, smacks into the (illumined) fridge and is now moving at such high speed that he just keeps on going, runs approximately a foot, vertically, up the fridge, then performs an impressive loop-the-loop, or a back flip, or whatever it is.

Wow.

A cat falls.

A shocked silence.

Wang Shu starts laughing.

Oh *shit*.

3.

ASK ME ABOUT MY VOW OF SILENCE

Avigail is – and has always been – fascinated by the power of silence. Over time this fascination has expanded – quite naturally – into an important, secondary belief in the comparative pointlessness of words. She quickly noticed how her sole designation in the noisy, chaotic home of her childhood (as the middle child of five) was simply to *peep-peep-peep* like a bird. She'd open her mouth to speak (that deep inhale on the cusp of the first syllable) only to be stuffed full of worms (and ignored). Children, she discovered, were sometimes listened to yet rarely heard.

And the emotions? Fruitless things – hurtful, burdensome things – always standing in the way of progress.

Another revelation was her capacity to befriend – better still, to harness – the very thing that was once imposed (un-heard-ness). Her power – such as it was – quickly became a defiant holding-in. A refusal to engage. But expressed so meekly, at first.

A gently tipped head. A cocked ear. Ah, to hear! To listen and remain quiet. To be lost-in-your-own-thoughts but still in charge of the map of meaning. To dumbly observe. To be *hush hush hush!* So exquisitely small! To take up such a tiny amount of space. To be so thoroughly modest and discreet and unassuming and … and … *la femme n'existe pas … il n'y a pas la femme.*

There is so much *room* in silence. It's so generous! It expands around you like a giant woollen blanket. Soft wool. Cosy. Quiet wool. Ah, the gorgeous feeling of semi-breath-holding. The sensual alertness of *not*. The resigned sigh of *shhhhhh*. The regretful silence. The watchful silence. The keen silence. The ambiguous silence. The mystery of silence. The infinite possibility of silence.
Everything so subtle. So gentle. Nothing stated, everything suggested.

Oooh, and the naughty waywardness of simply pointing, dumbly, when you *could* speak, but choose not to …

Avigail learned how to own her silence – how to protect it and to nurture it. She loved it. She hated the leaving of it – the bored croak of speech, the sudden colour and hurt and smash of language. Silence was thick, smooth cream. Words were a furious, fiery chilli sauce that hissed and raged and burned on the throat.

She once read a quotation by Max Picard about animals and silence: about how animals carry around a dense silence within them on behalf of man. Of how they are constantly placing down this silence in front of man.

A gift. An offering. A hope. A burden. A rebuke. An expectation.

Ahhh. Silence.
The thrill of it.

Avigail suspects that the great mission of her life will be to one day discover the full extent of this strange gift of hers – this amazing aptitude – for quiet. To test the seemingly endless parameters of ...
. . . .
. . . .
. . . .
. . . .
. . . .
. . . .
. . . .
. . . .

.... of...........................
....
...of...............   ....
....
....
....
...........of...................   ....
....
.............of..........   ....
....
....of..........................
....
....
....
of...........................of..............................
....
of............of.............. Sorry? *What?* Oh! Oh, I
couldn't *possibly* say!

Ah, this calculated regression!
This unanswerable *no*!

Although before all that, she needs to stop trying so
determinedly to be normal.

But she's worked so hard for it – starved for it. So she can't relinquish it. She must keep on pretending because she is so proud of her adaptation, of how good she has become at fitting in.

Seriously!
You would never know what a freak she truly is!
Surreptitiously.
Hidden away.
Underneath.

Perhaps the performance (the normality) is merely the set-up, and the punchline, the denouement, is unpronounced, is wordless?

Jouissance.

Even in the midst of tumult, there is quiet.
It hides in the top of her head. It is like a little golden frog, perpetually waiting to jump. It is ever watchful but makes no decisions. There is no 'do' or 'don't' here, no moral imperative. It is thoroughly dispassionate.
Tranquil.

'How about the tiles?' Charles asks. 'Do you like them?'

Charles's question can barely be heard above the desperate, harsh bark of Wang Shu's laughter.

Avigail stares at Charles, dumbfounded.
Wow.
Wow.
He really *is* a piece of work!

She replaces the silver cream jug (and the menstrual tea) back on to the refrigerator, then picks up the broom, the T-shirt (which Morpheus has happily relinquished) and retrieves Wang Shu's phone. She tries to pass Wang Shu the phone but Wang Shu is disabled by laughter. She has temporarily lost the use of her eight fingers. And her two thumbs.

Charles is now attempting to show Ying Yue the tiles, clearing away some of the assembled detritus. The tiles are quite repulsive. Over the terrifying howls of Wang Shu's laughter, Charles is pointing at the tiles and saying, 'These are the work of a celebrated designer called Alan Wallwork. My mother was very attached to them. It would be a great shame if whoever buys the house …'

Ying Yue is pinching her tiny, hardly chin and listening intently while nodding, thoughtfully.
'Beautiful!' she eventually pronounces.

Wang Shu suddenly stops laughing. Avigail (relieved) tries to pass her the phone again but Wang Shu flinches at Avigail's approach. Ying Yue (fighting the instinct to mirror) puts out *her* hand for the phone.
'Mother is afraid of the broom,' she gently explains. 'Being hit by a broom is very bad luck to a Chinese person and you were hit by the broom.'
Avigail is perplexed, 'So the broom is bad luck? Or am *I* now bad luck because I was hit by the broom which …?'
She is going to say 'which you knocked over', but resists the urge.
This is crazy.
She hands Ying Yue the phone.
Rather than answering Avigail's question, Ying Yue says something, brightly, to Wang Shu, in Chinese, while pointing to the wall tiles.

Wang Shu (like a toddler who has been momentarily distracted from its tantrum by a small bag of Cadbury's Chocolate Buttons) gazes at the tiles for a brief instant and then lets forth a loud stream of invective. Wang Shu plainly hates the tiles. The tiles have now come to represent everything about the falling broom that cannot be fully articulated in a European context. Ying Yue knocked the broom so is in disgrace. But the broom hit the Agent (Avigail). Yes! The broom hit the Agent! The Agent is jinxed! The viewing is jinxed. Then the Agent – with a complete lack of consideration and due care – allowed the broom to hit her toe! Wang Shu's toe! So Wang Shu's *toe* is jinxed! Which is horrifying! And disgusting! And the tiles are vile! *Damn* the tiles! *They* are jinxed. They are malodorous. They are despicable! The tiles are among the most revolting things Wang Shu has ever beheld in a life where much that is revolting has been beheld.

Wang Shu *loathes* the tiles.

Wang Shu continues this terrifying tirade, her lips flecked with spittle, her fists clenched (sometimes a fist briefly unclenches so a finger may point at her toe, then clenches again), for approximately a minute and a half.

When Wang Shu finishes speaking she promptly bursts into angry tears.

Yes. That's how deeply, deeply offended Wang Shu's *very essence* – her *very core* – is by the Alan Wallwork tiles.

Ying Yue bites her lip. Avigail looks at Charles.
Her eyes say: *What the fuck?!*
Charles shoves his hands into the pockets of his jeans.

Wang Shu's phone rings. Ying Yue immediately hands a sobbing Wang Shu the phone. Wang Shu takes the phone. Wang Shu instantly stops sobbing. Wang Shu answers the phone.
'*Ni hao?*'

Priorities.

Ying Yue promptly turns to Charles, her eyes dancing.
'Mother *loves* the tiles,' she beams.

Richard Grannon's sister once shared a piece of hippy-dippy shit with him – years ago – which he instantly discounted (having a residual suspicion of all things New Age) but later (against all his better instincts) felt compelled to re-evaluate, and then, eventually, to integrate it into his groundbreaking *Inner Critic* work. For no other reason than that it made a stupid kind of sense. Grannon's sister had learned this piece of wisdom from someone selling crystals at a festival (or a yoga teacher). It was presented in the form of a question. The question ran as follows:

'What is the story that you are living now about this situation?'

Again:

'What is the **story** that you are **living now**? About **this situation**?'

Is your truth simply a fiction?
Is the story that you are telling yourself – this flimsy, fragile, hashed-together fragment – all that you *truly* have?
If your answer to the last question is in the affirmative (and Charles's jury is currently still out on this), then it definitely needs to be a good one (a good story).

If the story is all you have –
then it needs to be a great story.

Charles looks at Ying Yue and he thinks, What is
the story that you are living now about this situation?
Ying Yue must be aware of the fact that he is aware
of the fact that she is lying about Wang Shu's feelings with regard to the Alan Wallwork tiles, but still,
still ...

What is Ying Yue's story? What story is she living
now?

?

These people are morons?

If I just say the right things – make the right noises
– it'll all be okay?

The world is simply a wild and delirious phantasm
(and I am a little feather floating though the cos-
mos)?

Charles scowls, and then wonders, What is the story that *I* – Charles – am living now about this situation?

Uh …

These people are morons?

If I just say the right things – make the right noises – it'll all be okay?

The world is simply a wild and mysterious phantasm (and if I could simply find the perfect toaster/kettle/juicer it'll all be dandy)?

How odd that he and Ying Yue (this strange, bedraggled, ill-drawn creature; this *girl*, part-stuffed, badly sewn, full of *otherness*) might actually be spinning *the same story*.

No!
No!!
Surely not?

He gazes at Ying Yue, owlishly.

There is something so plain, so empty, so smooth about Ying Yue's face that it is almost otherworldly. It *is* the face of a mammal, though. Yes. Just about. Ying Yue *is* a mammal. But oceanic. Cetacean. More like a dolphin than a person. Giant forehead. Tiny, friendly eyes. Dolphin smile. No chin. And her torso. Dolphin-shaped. Little arms like flippers.

Charles focuses in on Ying Yue's bandaged flipper. 'What actually happened to your flipper?' he wonders.
'Sorry?' Ying Yue's smile wavers.

Charles starts.

DID I ACTUALLY JUST SAY THAT?!

'WHAT ACTUALLY HAPPENED *TO YOUR FLIPPER?!*'

DID I ACTUALLY JUST SAY THAT?!

Out *loud?!*

'Have you ever considered covering your drying rack with a sheet?' Avigail interrupts. She is re-hanging the *arm bears* T-shirt. The offending broom has already been placed neatly out of harm's way. Avigail has a terrible feeling that the oyster shell hit and the broom fall may now spell disaster for the sale.

Yes.
Um ...

Hang on a second ...

Did Charles (illumined Charles) actually just utter the word 'flipper'?

Flipper?!

Avigail tries to re-run Charles's last sentence in her mind with a series of other words replacing flipper. But she can't. There aren't any other words to replace 'flipper'.

Hipper.
Chipper.
Clipper.
Tipper.

Flipper is a fairly particular word.

She visualises her commission going up in smoke.

Pouf!

Charles should actually be issued with a public health warning.
Charles is a *fucking menace.*

Flipper?!

Ying Yue touches her bad arm with her good hand and opens her mouth to speak but then defers, automatically, to Avigail.

Yet underneath …?

She is *seen*!
Ying Yue is seen!
And with flippers!
Ying Yue's spirit animal is the dolphin.
Ying Yue is *seen*!
By this strange-looking gentleman with his long, pale face and his holey, black underwear!

Flip-pers.
What mean this word?

La la la.

Charles glances over at Avigail.
What is the story that Avigail is living now about this situation?
he wonders.

Avigail is actually quoting the *Tao Te Ching* to herself.

There is no calamity
Like not knowing what is enough,
she thinks.

Fuck you, Charles,
she thinks.

Flipper?
she thinks.

The oyster shell?
she thinks.

The broom?
she thinks.

Avigail is living at least five different stories. And they are all running in her head, consecutively. And none of them fit perfectly together or make absolute sense.
But that's okay.
Yup. That's absolutely fine.

Because good enough is *more* than enough. For Avigail.

Ha.

Yeah.

If only.

4.

CAT HAIR IS LONELY PEOPLE GLITTER

But Lucy Molloy …? Who? Who she? Who Lucy Molloy? Heh?

Lucy Molloy doesn't own a cat. No. Lucy Molloy owns a tiny, ferocious Boston Terrier called Athena. Athena enjoys torturing small animals and large insects in Lucy Molloy's paved back garden in Perth, Australia. Lucy Molloy's current home is unfussy, white-walled and open-plan. She has a swimming pool. Lucy Molloy is in her mid-twenties and has glossy, straight dark brown hair. Lucy Molloy is very thin with larger than you'd expect, natural breasts. Lucy Molloy loves make-up. She obsesses over her brows and her lashes, although she isn't an especially girlie girl. Lucy Molloy relaxes at home in oversized T-shirts. She rides a motorcycle, but in a way that seems utterly devoid of swagger. Lucy Molloy wears glasses sometimes even though it's unlikely that there's anything wrong with her eyesight.

Lucy Molloy is married to the celebrated tattooist Dan Molloy. Dan Molloy tattooed her back with a huge, beautiful black and grey goddess Kali (the eyes staring, the tongue poking out). He also tattooed a knife on to her face. The handle hangs on her forehead, the blade disappears behind her eye and re-emerges on her cheek.

Dan Molloy's own face is also covered in tattoos. They're quite a startling couple to look at. But Lucy Molloy is, to all intents and purposes, one of the most conventional people you're ever likely to come across. Watching her posts on YouTube – about her collection of Harry Potter memorabilia or her online tube dress purchases or her love of stickers or how she makes vegan brownies (Lucy Molloy isn't vegan), or her trips to the beach or how she wants to get back into horse-riding – is like entering a realm of normalcy that is way beyond normal(cy). Lucy Molloy – she of the facial tattoo – celebrates an exquisite blandness. This is a real life that is utterly lacking in real-life anxieties. A drab, hallowed, exalted world that is strangely effortful in its effortlessness.

Oh, I promise I'll blog about my trip to the supermarket.

Oh, I didn't get around to it.

Oh, I can't be bothered putting any make-up on today.

This is how I dye my hair.

This is what I eat for breakfast.

I am dropping off my dry cleaning.

Is that a pimple on my cheek?

I am in the car driving to my husband's tattoo parlour so we can go out to dinner when he finishes up for the day ...

Lucy Molloy is everywoman.

Yes. This is the life Avigail should be living. This is the life she longs to live. The life of everywoman. But Lucy Molloy is already living this life, damn her. No existential anguish. No obsessive thoughts on global warming. Did that amazing cream blusher arrive in the mail from America yet? Shall we go out for waffles at the mall?

Avigail suspects Lucy Molloy's life feels rather like you're a large bluebottle happily drowning in a deliciously glittery pool of pineapple-flavour lipgloss.

Oh yes. The normal life. The sanctified life. This is the life Ying Yue should be living. If only Ying Yue could somehow contrive to wade across the perpetually gushing river of difference that appears to separate her from just about everyone else on the planet (and even from herself), then she too could have a life just like Lucy Molloy's. All her decisions so hugely small. All her challenges so magnificently minimal. All her thoughts so deliciously curtailed. This gorgeous, shimmering myopia. This weirdly disgruntled bland-happy-different-same-pretty-unchallenging-modern-unthinking-blinkered-independent-unblinkered-sort-of-free-unfree-impossibly-possibly-laundry-Disney-Channel-waxing-friends-tapas-fill the car with diesel etc. life.

Does Lucy Molloy know that your true peace and your true joy are uncaused?

Huh?

Does Lucy Molloy know that life consists of beauty-terror-knowledge (aka desire-suffering-enlightenment)?

Huh?

It's unlikely.

She has no *need* to know.

Because she is blessed.

Blessed.

If only Avigail and Ying Yue knew that they were both worshippers at the altar of Lucy Molloy – that the diverse/magical/complex patterns of their individual lives converge and are conjoined within the singular persona of Lucy Molloy – how different this all might be. The vibe. The mood. The exchanges. The atmosphere. Everything. But they don't know. And they are unlikely to find out because there are now only eight short minutes still remaining of this particular house viewing.

Oh my.

7.59

And counting.

Richard Grannon likes to repeat the phrase ONLY DEAD FISH GO WITH THE FLOW.

Richard Grannon believes it's good to buck the system. To think out of the box.

Richard Grannon does not approve of religion. He thinks religion is just an excuse not to take ownership of your own life and destiny. He loosely associates it with the dread concept of 'magical thinking'. Although he does believe in something he calls '*semangat*' which is a Malay word that refers to a kind of mind energy, a sort of positive, humming, joyful inner song.

Hang on ...
It's that time again! Charles really needs to check in on his emotions (even if he doesn't really believe that he *has* any – even then).

How is Charles feeling?

How are you feeling, Charles?

Um.

Charles feels:

Weird.
Flustered.
Open.
Warm.
Creaky.
Itchy.
Confused.

'A sheet? Why would I hang a sheet over the drying rack?' he wonders.

Slightly snarky.

Flippers?!

'That's kind of the whole point,' Avigail sighs (Oh the boredom of explaining the sodding obvious: This is my *whole life*, she thinks, just explaining the sodding obvious. Over and over and over. WITH *BASTARD WORDS*). 'For the rack to work efficiently the whole thing needs to be enclosed.'

'But it works perfectly well without a sheet,' Charles persists. 'My mother never used a sheet.'

'It's just common sense, Charles.' Avigail smiles (with terrific insincerity). 'If you do your bedding in the first wash you can hang it over the rack and create a vacuum to hold in the heat. Then, after you've done the remainder of your laundry, in a second wash, you can place your T-shirts and vests etc. *inside* and not only keep the heat contained – which is more environmental – but save money and speed up the drying process to boot.'

The electric drying rack is illumined.

Everything is illumined.

Even the T-shirt Ying Yue is currently gazing at, dazedly, which reads: **Cat hair is lonely people glitter.** *Even that T-shirt is illumined.*

'If the manufacturers wanted you to cover it then surely they would've provided a cover *with* the rack?' Charles argues.

Charles thinks Avigail is one of the *least sincere* people he has ever met.

'You don't need a cover,' Avigail explains AGAIN (He *has* to be kidding. Honestly. He *has* to be kidding). 'You use your sheets – your bed linen to cover the rack. Wet or dry. It's just lateral thinking. It's just basic common sense.'
Charles glares at Avigail.

Basic common sense?!

'And I think you'll find it's actually more decorous to do it that way,' she adds. 'More modest.'

Decorous?
Avigail winces the instant she finishes speaking. She winces at herself.
Modest?

Who *is* this stranger person mouth talking?

What the heck?!

Am going losing mind totally.

Charles glares at Avigail.

Decorous?
Modest?!

Is Avigail actually standing there, in *his* kitchen, accusing *him* – Charles – of being *in*decorous? Of being *im*modest?
(Angry voice.)

Um.

Perhaps Avigail is simply standing there, in *his* kitchen, advising *him* (Charles) of a better way – a more efficient way – to use his electric drying rack?
(Rational voice.)

Pause.

No. Seriously. Is Avigail actually standing there, in *his* kitchen, accusing *him* – Charles – of being *in*decorous? Of being *im*modest?

Finding *fault* with him? *Undermining* him? *Ridiculing* him?

HOW DARE SHE?

HOW *DARE* SHE?

HOW *DARE* SHE?!

This seemingly disproportionate response to Avigail's comments re the rack is no longer really about Avigail – *or* the drying rack – is it?

No …

Oh. um … Hello? Hi! It's lil' ol' me again!

I am an emotional flashback!

I am an emotional flashback!

I am an emotional flashback!

Panic alarm goes off.

Weee-wahh-weee-wahh-weee-wahh!

Emotional flashback politely proffers Charles its magnificently red-satin-begloved paw.

Gulp.

Richard Grannon has taught Charles to recognise the emotional flashback.

I am making progress!
I embrace change!

Argh. That familiar, hot feeling of rage washing over him. That constricted sensation in his throat and his chest. That surge of blind, condensed *fury.*

Richard Grannon – on numerous occasions – has respectfully pointed his YouTube followers in the direction of Pete Walker's seminal book *Complex PTSD: From Surviving to Thriving* (not forgetting his earlier, groundbreaking text *The Tao of Fully Feeling*) available free on Amazon Kindle, Charles has noted, if you are able to work out what the hell signing up to it actually means for your long-term fiscal and psychological well-being (which Charles isn't, so he has purchased both, at inordinate expense, in paperback).

It was Pete Walker – an American therapist – who first made the connection between Post Traumatic Stress Disorder (typically experienced by war veterans with its characteristic mental flashbacks – triggered seemingly at random or by certain stressful situations) and *Complex* PTSD/R where the victim experiences *emotional* flashbacks. This means that they don't have visions, as such, but they are engulfed/ obliterated by feelings instead. These feelings are distorting, panic-inducing, arbitrary, overwhelming.

The original cause of these 'emotional' flashbacks isn't as pointed and specific as in the standard PTSD (i.e. one, specific traumatic incident). They are sourced in a kind of watercolour wash – a destabilising blur – of traumatic experiences (generally associated with long-term physical and/or emotional childhood abuse: neglect, harsh criticism, cruelty, mixed-messages, parental unreliability/unpredictability). Over time this wash of abuse effects the brain's HPA axis (these are the glands that relate to threat perception) and the individual's baseline state becomes dis-

regulated – fluctuates and nose-dives with no percep-
tible external cause. The primitive parts of the brain
responsible for fight/flight responses are perpetually over-stimulated. The person is then emotionally
hyper-normalised. They try to stop feeling (feelings are
at once utterly overwhelming and completely unreli-
able). They try to block these unwelcome responses
and end up over-thinking things or simply checking
out. Feelings become the enemy. Feelings attack. They
must be repressed. They become dangerous and
unpredictable.

There is so much Charles still has to learn.

The Toxic Inner Critic.
Perfectionism.
The Trauma Tunnel.
Entitlement.
Emotional dis-regulation.
Developing critical thinking skills.
Learned Responses.
S.N.A.F.U. (situation-normal-all-fucked-up)
The Somatic Body.
Semangat.
Emotional flashbacks.

If only he could get started!

Why, why, why can't I get started?

Although he *does* know about the Hand Mnemonic.
He has almost got the Hand Mnemonic down pat.
It's a part of the basic skill-set that Grannon introduced, online, and in seminars, during an earlier
phase (before the big American backers got on
board and encouraged him to stop doing too much
for free and being such a wildman/smart-arse).

Ah. The inter-relatedness of things. Yes.
There's always something else.
Isn't there?
Something else?
To look for?
Must. Find. Something. Else.
Easier.
Quicker.
Cheaper.
Better.
Searching.
For something else.
An add-on.

A bonus-ball.

To make it okay.

To feed the hunger.

To block that GIANT GAPING MAW inside that longs to be filled but cannot be filled.

Empty.

Just a massive vacuum within inhabited by a swarm of anxiously buzzing bees.

What's next?

What's next?

*In*decorous?

*Imm*odest?

Fuck Avigail! Screw her!

The emotional flashback is seductive. But it isn't real. It is just a learned response. Grannon compares it to a looping tape that is suddenly triggered and then starts playing in the mind (trots out a familiar, painful tune) but has no useful purpose. It's exaggerated. It's ultimately destructive. It simply generates anxiety and pain. It's anti-social. It's inappropriate. It's infantilising. Worst of all, it's self-sabotaging.

His cruel Inner Critic compels Charles to remain at the approximate developmental age of a fourteen-year-old boy.

Charles is the Peter Pan of the emotions.

(Hello?
Hello?
Where Tinkerbell?)

When Avigail recommends that Charles covers his drying rack with a sheet, Charles's mind flashes back (without him knowing it, because the flashback is emotional, not intellectual) to the time (the many times) that his father, Barri, humiliated him by announcing to his extended family, during the evening meal, that he shouldn't be allowed orange cordial with his food (he never *asked* for cordial! He never asked for it – even though he was thirsty! Even though he was bone dry!) because he was still pissing the bed. Charles wet the bed in his father's house on weekend visits because he was too frightened to get up and go to the toilet at night after he'd flushed on one occasion and had been slapped for waking his grandfather (whose bedroom was adjacent to the toilet). And then, when he didn't flush, he had been attacked and ridiculed for being dirty and bad-mannered and ill-bred.

'This may be acceptable in Bulgaria,' his father's first/only wife hissed, pointing angrily into the golden bowl (Charles held firmly by the collar of his pyjama top, his three half-brothers sniggering in the background), 'but it *isn't* acceptable here.'

TRI BRAWD!
TRI BRAWD!
TRI BRAWD!

That's what Charles feels when Avigail calls him immodest. All the anxiety. All the ridicule. All the humiliation of his father's earlier attacks.

Six minutes remaining.

Avigail is saying something.
Charles tries to −

106

SHAME!

tune in −

HUMILIATION!

over the blare of his −

FURY!

emotional flashback.

There is the sound of something falling in another room.

EH?

'Is the cat okay, do you think?' Avigail is wondering. 'She took quite a tumble before ...'

She?
SHE?!

What is it with this infernal woman and *she?* Charles asks himself.

Meanwhile, he is surreptitiously tapping the thumb of his left hand (the left is his dominant hand) with a finger of his right.

I AM KING OF MY OWN SERENITY
I AM THE RULER OF MYSELF . . .

he intones, visualising a crown,

I AM SOVEREIGN,

he intones.

Tap, tap, tap on the thumb.

I AM SOVEREIGN.

Next, the index finger –

Tap tap tap . . .

WITH THIS, MY INDEX FINGER, I AM POINTING AT THE INNER CRITIC – THE NEGATIVE, 'PARENT' VOICE – I AM POINTING AT HIM AND IDENTIFYING HIM.

GET LOST!
I WILL *NOT* BE ATTACKED AND DOMI-
NATED BY YOU ANY LONGER ...

Tap tap tap ...

Next the middle finger ...

tap tap tap ...

LEARN HOW TO SAY NO!
BE BOUNDARIED!
SAY *NO* TO THE INNER CRITIC.
SAY *NO* TO YOURSELF.
BE MENTALLY STRONG!
AND DON'T BE AFRAID TO SAY *NO* TO
OTHER PEOPLE, EITHER! WITHOUT FLIN-
CHING! BOLDLY. UNAPOLOGETICALLY.
BETTER STILL, WITH A SMILE ...

'The cat's fine,' he mutters.

Wang Shu is talking on the phone in Chinese. As
she talks, though (presumably in an unconscious
attempt to distract herself from the broom/toe

trauma), she is casually busying herself with other stuff. Initially she takes a couple of the herbal teas down from the top of the refrigerator and sniffs them, sceptically. The Fennel Tea disgusts her. The Turmeric and Ginger Tea succeeds in not entirely provoking her ire. Next Wang Shu opens the refrigerator and looks inside. There are three types of live probiotic yoghurt on the top shelf. All are out of date. Wang Shu picks one up and holds it, quizzically, to the light. She winces. She returns it from whence it came. Next Wang Shu smells the milk. She winces again and casually carries the milk over to the sink as she talks on the phone in Chinese.

'Zonggong duoshao qian?'

. . .

'Huh?'

. . .

'Duoshao?!'

Charles says – almost to himself – 'I actually just bought that milk this morning.' Wang Shu pours the milk down the sink. She then returns the carton to the fridge and continues to inspect the fridge's contents. She pulls out some broccoli and smells it.

110

She shakes her head. She places the broccoli down on the counter and then indicates over her shoulder (presumably to Ying Yue) that she needs some assistance.

Ying Yue bows slightly (it's more a curtsey than a bow, really) first to Charles, then to Avigail. 'Is this refrigerator to be included in sale?' she tentatively asks.

'I haven't quite decided,' Charles admits (the refrigerator is not included in the sale).

People who suffer from porous internal boundaries because of a history of abuse find it virtually impossible to say 'no'.

It's JUST TOO HARD!

I ... I ... I ... I ... *can't!*

Tap tap tap ...

LEARN HOW TO SAY NO!
BE BOUNDARIED!
SAY *NO* TO THE INNER CRITIC.
SAY *NO* TO YOURSELF.

BE MENTALLY STRONG!
AND DON'T BE AFRAID TO SAY *NO* TO
OTHER PEOPLE, EITHER! WITHOUT FLIN-
CHING! BOLDLY. UNAPOLOGETICALLY.
WITH A SMILE ...

Wang Shu indicates – more aggressively now – that
she needs assistance (still talking in Chinese, still
facing into the open fridge). Ying Yue shuffles over to
her mother's side. Wang Shu points to the broccoli.
Ying Yue *wants* to stop her mother from behaving
inappropriately but she CANNOT SAY NO to
Wang Shu. She is Wang Shu's echo, her mirror,
after all. Ying Yue grabs a hold of the broccoli. She
presses her lips together, agonised. She swallows,
nervously. She inhales. She holds her breath. She
turns around. She carries the broccoli over to the
bin (where Charles still stands). Even though Ying
Yue is holding her breath (so is now – to all intents
and purposes – completely invisible), Charles finds
himself ...

LEARN HOW TO SAY NO! BE BOUNDARIED!

Tap tap tap ...

… pressing down on to the bin pedal with his foot. The bin lid swings open …

The pedal bin is illumined.

The broccoli is illumined.

Ying Yue (still holding her breath), gently drops the (illumined) broccoli into the (illumined) pedal bin. It nestles up against the bloodied tissue and the cellophane wrapper of a value pack of jotters (unlined. Illumined). Charles releases the pedal. Ying Yue exhales.

Avigail finds Charles's patent lack of concern for his cat deeply perturbing. She has no idea why she suddenly keeps gendering everything female. She knows that the cat is called Morpheus and Morpheus is a boy's name, isn't it?

Isn't it?

The Greek god of dreams?

Ah …

The River of Forgetfulness?
The River of Oblivion?

That elusive guy in the *Matrix* films?

Avigail also has no idea how she might stop Wang Shu from emptying out Charles's fridge. She is slightly concerned that stopping someone from emptying out a stranger's fridge may be bad luck to the Chinese. Although (curiously) she suddenly remembers how empty things (an empty stove, an empty bucket, an empty house) are considered unlucky by Jews.

Avigail wonders what is *good* luck to the Chinese (aside from the number 8)?

She is also perturbed by Ying Yue's breath-holding which strikes her as quite odd. She is unable to fully grasp the complexities of Ying Yue's relationship with Wang Shu, but she suspects that it isn't entirely functional or tremendously nurturing.
Ying Yue reminds her of an exhausted marsupial.

'Ying Yue,' Avigail asks, 'what, aside from the number 8, is *good* luck in Chinese culture?'

Ying Yue pauses mid-way between the refrigerator and the pedal bin. She is clutching a mouldy block of cheese which Wang Shu has just handed her. Ying Yue is holding her breath so kind of imagines that Avigail can't see her.

Hmm. This is complex. Does she exhale and answer, or does she try to answer while still holding her breath?

She isn't sure.

Charles (as if sensing Ying Yue's disquiet) silently opens the pedal bin.

Fourth finger … tap tap tap … ring finger … tap tap tap …

MUST SELF-PARTNER …

Tap tap tap …

Ying Yue takes this as a sign. She throws the cheese into the bin:

a hit!

then exclaims, very quickly, in a single, breathy expulsion:

'Uh … colour red – lucky colour … auspicious … wedding colour …

uh … lucky dragon …

uh … turtle …

yes … venerable turtle lives to great age …

uh … lucky fish … for wealth … for abundance …

and uh … lucky circle – always round shape is very propitious …

uh … lucky oranges … uh … word for orange is same-like as word for lucky and same-like as word for gold and gold is always lucky …

Uh … yes … lucky turtle … for long life …

Uh …'

Her eyes frantically scan the room, hunting for inspiration.

'*In the Ancient East there is a dragon ... she is called China –*
We are all descendants of the dragon.'

Ying Yue begins to sing; she has an oddly haunting, reedy, keening voice.
Ying Yue sings in Chinese. It is a traditional song which she only really knows because it has been reworked by the ridiculously handsome American-Chinese pop star/film star/environmental activist Wang Leehom. If Avigail or Charles could speak any Chinese they would hear:

> *In the Far East there is a river,*
> *its name is the Yangtze River*
> *In the Far East there is a river,*
> *its name is the Yellow River*

> *Although I've never seen the beauty of the Yangtze,*
> *in my dreams I miraculously travel the Yangtze's waters*
> *Although I've never heard the strength of the Yellow River,*
> *the rushing and surging waters are in my dreams ...*

'*YING YUUUUUUUUUUUE!*' Wang Shu suddenly bellows, slamming the fridge shut with a violent smack:

'CAN' YOU *HEA'* I ON THE FUCKING *PHONE*?!'

5.

SORRY I'M LATE, BUT I DIDN'T WANT TO COME

As Ying Yue sings, Avigail (disarmed and horrified in equal measure) instantly forges a series of cultural connections. She remembers the Evil Eye and the lengths her *bubbeh* would go to in order to confound its wicked machinations …

The little red strings tied around their wrists.

Spitting three times (*psi! psi! psi!*) and hissing *kinehore* whenever she mentioned anything good happening (bragging was considered unwise – certainly unattractive – even dangerous).

Salt in the corners of the rooms in new houses or in the pockets of new clothes.

A safety pin pushed under a shirt collar before a long trip.

119

(Metal was always considered lucky because the Hebrew for iron – *barzel* – is an acronym of the names of the mothers of the Children of Israel:

Billhook
Rachel
Zilch
Leah ...)

Windows always propped very slightly ajar so that evil spirits might make their escape.

Holy books always kept very firmly shut so that evil spirits mightn't gain access.

The lucky number 18 – *chai* – the lowest emanation of *Elohim*.

Oh yes, *sneezing*; both as a grave omen and as a powerful indicator of a profound truth recently uttered.

It all comes flooding back.

Home.

Ouch.

How raw that word feels. How sharply this briefest of syllables cuts. Such a savage noun.

Avigail vaguely recalls being taught about how the world was created from the twenty-two Hebrew letters – in ten speeches by *Elohim*. Yes. Ten speeches which – altogether – combined to contain everything there is. All ramifications of things. Each possibility. Every iteration. So the world was born of words. These simple twenty-two letters; the humble building blocks of the universe.

Avigail also remembers the curious story of how the letters arrived in reverse order, *Tav* to *Aleph* with *Bet* – the second from first and therefore second from last – meaning *Berachah* (a blessing) demanding, perhaps vaingloriously, that he might be given the honour of creating the world (or starting the Torah – which was, in effect, the same thing). *Elohim* cordially agreed, but then the first/last letter, *Aleph*, stood aside, piqued, and refused to appear before *Elohim* because *Bet* has already won the greatest prize of all the letters. *Elohim* called *Aleph* forward, and, eventually (rather sullenly), he came. *Elohim* then told *Aleph* that he should not worry, because he, *Aleph*, would stand at the head of all the letters and that all unity would be found in him alone.

The first of the seventy names of God will begin, silently, with *Aleph*.

Ahhh ... *Elohim*.

He is the Power.
God of Gods.

Aleph makes no sound. *Aleph*, like Avigail, is the brief inhale before anything might properly be uttered.

Aleph is also the letter of *fire*. He stands proudly at the head of the word, fire. He is the oxygen that feeds the fire and lets it burn. Although his is a fire that dances and flickers and flames but never harms or destroys.

The primordial fire.

Home.

Bet, strangely, is the letter that represents place, that represents home; it is grounded, of the earth, and the *dagesh* – or dot – hidden within is the one who lives inside it.

The one who belongs.

Avigail suddenly sees her own turmoil – her own battle – neatly expressed in these two Hebrew letters – *Bet* and *Aleph* – savagely competing against each other ...
Yet *Elohim* establishes peace between them, does he not?

Avigail scowls and thinks about everything feeling topsy-turvy from the very outset ...

Home.

But then wasn't the Torah started on the last page and completed on the first? And the letters? Everything back-to-front, inside-out, arse over tit?

Avigail ponders her own strange journey from silence to sound, from sound to silence.

Was it such a strange journey after all?

Perhaps I am not the silence that follows, she muses, the silence imposed, the quietening down, but rather – like *Aleph* – the letter who stands apart and will not immediately enter (*defiant Aleph!*) – the deep inhale *before* ...

Perhaps, she thinks, there is room for me after all? A home. Perhaps I only had to stand outside a while and quietly wait for my number to be called?

Avigail remembers the old story of how *Elohim* actually created twenty-three letters – but the twenty-third letter had somehow gone missing. This extraordinary, elusive, staggeringly lovely consonant, lost.

Where is the lost letter?
Where?
Where?
And what's its shape?
And what's its sound?

And when it is found? Ah. All the world's troubles and mis-fires and imperfections – all strife and

disorder – will finally be set to rights in a cacoph-
ony of new words and new sentences and new
works, not hitherto conceived of.

Yes. Everything falling neatly into place, the very
instant this lost letter is uttered.

Perhaps we all have the lost letter written in our
hearts, Avigail ponders, and it just needs to be
searched for and then somehow articu- ... articula
... spoken?

Avigail feels her pages turning backwards. She
hears the impatient licking of dry forefingers and
thumbs, the rustle of expectation.

Something *must* be said!

Surely?

Something curious and exceptional and thoroughly
singular!

Something new.

Born of her own, *very particular*, experience.

Oh, but ...
But *what?*
And *when?*
And *how?*

And *to whom* exactly*?*

This is to be her mission, surely? To discover?
To peek around her? To stand and wait? To forge
her lips into an apparently unfamiliar shape?

Yes.

And look!

Look!

Finally!

Avigail is illumined.

6.

I RUN WITH SCISSORS

Charles sneezes. It's very possible that he's allergic to Ying Yue's singing. Or possibly to Wang Shu's shouting. Or – by Avigail's *bubbeh*'s calculations – a profound truth has just been uttered or (perhaps, more ominously) a grave omen is being augured.

Charles doesn't give a damn about any of this because he is still tapping away at his fourth finger:

MUST SELF-PARTNER!

Yes! Yes!

I AM SOVEREIGN.
I AM SOVEREIGN.
I AM SOVEREIGN.

Say *anything* enough times and it becomes true. Doesn't it?

When you self-partner, it's kind of like marrying yourself. As he taps, Charles imagines a wedding band encircling his ring finger (just as Richard Grannon suggested he might).

Must be here – <u>for myself</u>.
Because if I can't be here – <u>for myself</u> – why on earth should anyone else bother being here – <u>for me</u>?

If *I* can't?

If *I* can't be here – <u>for myself</u>?

Why should anyone else bother?

Being here?

<u>For me</u>?

An important constituent of Grannon's *Silencing the Inner Critic* course involves doing something called 'Re-patterning the Inner Parent'.
Charles has not watched this particular module the whole way through – or even partially – but he *has* cast a jittery eye over the module's full transcript

to steel himself against the possibility that Richard Grannon might say something in the video that offends his – Charles's – delicate sensibilities about, uh, not sure what, exactly, but, um, he's hyper, *hyper* sensitive and he *loathes* surprises ...

And he is already steeling himself for disappointment. He is patiently awaiting disillusionment. He's almost ... it would be wrong to say that he is anticipating it – looking forward to it, *hoping* for it – but, yes, he is definitely steeling himself for it.

Is this self-sabotage?
Surely not?

There is only room for one moronic idealist in Charles's life.
And that one moronic idealist is Charles himself.
Charles can always depend upon his dreadfully fucked-up idealistic self to make dreadfully fucked-up idealistic decisions.

Richard Grannon is bound to *let him down*.
Just like everybody else does/will/always has.
It's pretty much inevitable.
It's a foregone conclusion.

So ... yes, *very* broadly speaking (from what Charles can deduce), this 're-patterning' involves conceptualising two perfect parents and then employing a series of simple, psychological ruses to gradually retrain the mind into being less critical and more nurturing. So the Bad Parent (the Inner Critic – the Toxic Super-Ego) slowly becomes a Good Parent (or Parent-s).

Charles will be required to imagine a perfect parent (two perfect parents) and to list (in his notebook) what he thinks their ideal characteristics might be.

Um ...

Charles thinks it's important for a perfect parent to be:

Consistent.

Respectful.

Honest.

Present.

Generous.

Kind.

Loving.

Tender.

Unflinching.

Responsive.

Authentic.

Forgiving.

Creative.

Accepting.

Non-judgemental.

Sympathetic.

Brave.

Patient.

Supportive (did he already say that?).

Warm.

Open.

Fun.

Like Barack and Michelle Obama.

Michelle and Barack are Charles's perfect parents.

The two-year-old Charles sits happily on Michelle Obama's warm lap as she gently plaits his hair (although anyone who plaits knows that this process is never gentle) into fastidiously neat lines of corn-rows.

Hmm. That's a slightly odd and unsettling fantasy.

For a 40 y/o man.

Barack . . .

Ah, Barack.
Barack takes Charles to the Oval Office and lets
Charles sit on the President's chair. And answer the
President's phone.

Yes.

And he pats Charles supportively on the shoulder.
And he says things like: 'You don't need to buy that
second-hand juicer because you are *already good
enough*, Son.'

Barack thinks that Charles is perfect *just as he is*.

Barack and Michelle wouldn't change so much as *a
single hair* on Charles's head.

Charles thinks Ying Yue's singing voice is utterly
bizarre. *Haunting.*
Like windscreen wipers being operated at full pelt
when there hasn't been any rain and the windscreen
is still bone dry.
Squeaky.
Very odd.

Ying Yue gazes up at the ceiling when she sings (so she can remember the words).
Isn't that what angels do? When they sing? Charles thinks. Don't angels look upwards – heavenwards – angelically – while they sing – just like she does?

Ooh. Alien thought.

Stop it.

Fucking *angels.*

Next it'll be fucking *unicorns.*

Fuck off.
Fuck *off.*

Fucking *angels.*

Wang Shu is talking on the phone in Chinese.
Avigail is frowning and staring off into the middle distance.
(Probably silently plotting what – or who – she can arbitrarily re-gender next, Charles muses.)

How am I feeling? Charles wonders.

Panicked.
Confused.
Breathless.
Slightly constipated.

Is constipation an emotion, though? Strictly speaking?

'Slightly constipated' could be a *metaphor*, Charles supposes, a metaphor for something like … uh … general unease. For a blocked-ness. A resistance. To THE NEW.

Yeah.

Must embrace THE NEW.

Must stop being such a grouchy, closed-down, pent-up old duffer.

Glass half empty.

Perpetually defensive.

Suspicious.

Did you know that the most valuable human qual-ity/virtue (of all human qualities/virtues) is ...

FLEXIBILITY?

!

Not bravery.
Not loyalty.
Not kindness.
Not generosity.

No.

Flexibility.

Did you know that?

Jesus was incredibly flexible. Always innovating Jewish traditions.
Buddha promoted the middle way.
Sri Ramakrishna was like a kid in a sweetshop.
Eckhart Tolle giggles a lot.

I am receptive.

I am flexible.

I am open to change.

After bellowing at Ying Yue to stop her dreadful singing, Wang Shu has once again retreated into the familiar space – the gap – between the refrigerator and the kitchen door so that she might give her full attention to the **VERY IMPORTANT** conversation she is having (in Chinese) on her mobile phone.

Ying Yue is gazing intently at Charles as if awaiting a cue.

Ying Yue *is* awaiting a cue from Charles. Ying Yue likes this tall, ancient man with his many locks on the front door and the sometimes bits of holes in his underpants and his great facility to open and close bins and his pointless affection for dreadful tilework. What will Charles do next? Ying Yue wonders. She is in complete awe of his spontaneity. Charles appears infinitely surprising to her.

So tall!

Ying Yue is impressed by everyone. But at this precise moment in time she is impressed by Charles.

Charles?
Charl-sss?
Cha-ruls?

What Char-uls do now?
Huh?
Why Char-uls tapping-tapping-tapping his finger so much?
Arthritis?
How interesting!
Splitter-splatter old fat stains on the ceiling.
Pinched toe in shoe.
Hmm.
Could save cheese if cut off mouldy bit, maybe?

Ying Yue peers around her, myopically (Ying Yue is not short-sighted, but she affects short-sightedness because objects in the world are often very surprising to her – *door! hand! kitchen blind!* – and she needs to protect herself from the shock of it all). Ying Yue is looking for a sharp knife. Ying Yue sees a blunt butter-style knife on the draining board. She grabs it. She then

138

opens the lid of the bin (manually) and reaches deep inside. She feels around for a while. She finally locates the pat of cheese (which – due to its weight – has fallen to the bottom of the bin). Ying Yue carries the cheese (a medium-strength Tesco own-brand Cheddar) to the counter and pushes a couple of objects out of the way (a new copy of *JapanEasy* by Tim Anderson, a new pair of black, silicone, mini-mitt-style oven gloves). Ying Yue opens the packet, removes the small block of cheese and carefully chops the mouldy segment off, then tosses it into the bin, returns the non-mouldy remainder back to its bag, seals it, picks it up, delightedly, and presents it to Char-uls.

Char-uls takes the proffered cheese. Ying Yue beams and bows.

Charles is unsure of what to do next.

What is the appropriate form of behaviour/ response when a visitor to your home throws away something from your fridge and then retrieves it again from the bin and returns it to you, proudly (*sans* mould)?

'I like cheese,' Charles says, limply.

Charles might as well have said, 'Whistle hairpin kangaroo.'

It's just noise. It's just some idiotic syllables tumbling out of his mouth after a brief flirtation with his brain, his voice box and his tongue.

'Me too!!' Ying Yue applauds Char-uls. The man is a genius!

Ying Yue is bewitched by Char-uls. Right this very minute. While her eyes are fixed upon him. Bewitched!

In thirty seconds' time Ying Yue will be bewitched by a cracked floor tile which from a certain angle looks like a mountain being struck by a bolt of lightning.

Although – to be perfectly honest – Ying Yue doesn't actually like cheese that much. But she is willing to like cheese if Char-uls likes cheese. Charles doesn't actually like cheese all that much, either. But he couldn't think of anything else to say. And Ying Yue is so delighted by Charles's profession of 'like' for cheese that Charles is almost willing to believe that he *does* like cheese.

The creature in the house who *authentically* likes cheese is Morpheus who in actual fact *loves* cheese and this is why Charles buys cheese and uses it to create a malleable and edible yeasty shell around the assorted tablets (Tenormin, Inderal, Dilacor XR) used in the treatment of his Hypertrophic Cardiomyopathy. What Charles doesn't know is that Morpheus suffers from Hypertrophic Cardiomyopathy *simply because* he wants cheese so badly. Charles's mother, Branimira, always fed Morpheus cheese. For Morpheus, cheese represents Branimira's love.

Branimira was Morpheus's perfect parent.

And now she is gone.

Charles is uncertain what to do with the cheese. He doesn't feel he can put it straight back into the refrigerator again, so he pats it, approvingly, then pushes it into his trouser pocket.

'It's actually inadvisable to keep cheese in plastic,' Avigail volunteers. 'It needs to breathe. If a plastic wrap is too tight the cheese is way more likely to develop bacteria.'

Ying Yue turns to inspect Avigail. Ying Yue is deeply impressed by Avigail's insights into cheese preservation.

Charles turns to inspect Avigail. Charles is borderline hostile to Avigail's insights into cheese preservation. No. He isn't borderline. He is *actively* hostile.

Fucking know-it-all.

'Cheese automatically produces ammonia,' Avigail continues, 'it's a natural by-product of cheese and it needs to be released. The plastic interferes with this. For that reason you're much better off storing cheese in parchment or wax paper.'

'Parchment?!' Charles jeers. He is visualising vellum. Cheese in vellum?
Ridiculous!

Charles strongly suspects that Avigail is both a fat-head and a perfectionist. He can see — in Avigail — what an insidious and abhorrent trait perfectionism is. Not only insidious and abhorrent but unattractive. Perfectionism is signally unattractive.

If Charles didn't dislike/fear Avigail so much he would actually pity her.

But pity is exhausting and he needs to partner *himself* right now. He needs to be practising *self-*compassion.

I mean why was she hiding behind a wall earlier? (Avigail. The wall. Earlier.)
Is it appropriate for an estate agent to leave a property mid-viewing and then hide behind a wall on an adjacent street?

Charles despairs for Avigail.

What am I feeling? Charles asks himself.

Pity (for Avigail. He can't help it. Poor thing. He pities her).

Guilty (for saying he likes cheese when he doesn't like cheese. Although he doesn't *dis*like cheese. He is indifferent to cheese. Surely this is people-pleasing by any other name? Surely this is fawning? Am I flight, freeze, *fawn* after all? Charles wonders).

Bemused (cheese in pocket feels awkward and slightly cold against thigh).

Worried (strange noises coming from direction of living room/work room).

'So I think we've probably got the sum of the kitchen by now,' Avigail says, satisfied that she has offered all the information she currently possesses on the packaging of cheese (although she has plenty more to say on the storage of cheese, in general). 'Shall we head through to the living room? Uh ... *yes* ...? Everyone?'

Nobody reacts.

The 'everyone' is mainly directed towards Wang Shu. But Wang Shu has no intention of interrupting her important phone call (in Chinese) so turns her back on Avigail and talks MORE LOUDLY THAN EVER into her phone. Wang Shu is now facing the wall which Avigail is pretty sure (in ALL cultures) means 'screw you'.

There is a brief pause as Avigail ponders how best to negotiate this situation. During this hiatus there is the sound of something being violently shoved or knocked over in an adjacent room.

That's weird!

What mean could this the hell?

Charles has been busily trying to *'feel the feels'* (as Grannon so delightfully and seductively puts it). He has been distracted.

68.9 per cent distracted.

Emotions are very time/energy/thought-consuming things.

But ...

Huh?!

He snaps to attention.

Ooh. What story is Charles living now about this situation?

Bailiff? Feline madness? Earthquake?

Well, *whatever* the story Charles is living now about this situation –

Poltergeist?

– it is 99.9 per cent unlikely that his story (creative as he undoubtedly is, inventive as he undoubtedly is) involves a fiercely intelligent, immaculately attired, twenty-three-year-old Ethiopian professional carer called Gyasi 'Chance' Ebo riffling furiously though his teddy bear collection.

Because that's the story *we* are living now about this situation.

Not Charles.

Because that's *the* story.

But hey.

emoji of shrugging person

Charles quickly jinks past Ying Yue (who – traumatised by her mother's rudeness – is displacing her anxiety into holding her breath and inspecting a cracked kitchen floor tile) and charges out of the room towards the kerfuffle.

Avigail turns to follow Charles.

There are now approximately 4.12 minutes remaining of this house viewing.

Morpheus (meanwhile) has sneaked his way into the spare bedroom (someone has left the door open) and is taking an illicit dump in the oversized plant pot of a large, slightly yellowing Calathea Whitestar. He is thinking about cheese, even now. Even as he strains. But then Morpheus is *always* thinking about cheese, near enough.

Morpheus is focused.
Morpheus is calm.
Morpheus is goal-driven.

Morpheus is '*getting shit done*'.

Go, Morpheus.

We apologise, in advance, for the brief interruption . . .

*. . . but it is necessary at this moment in the novella (hence-forth referred to as I Am Sovereign) to warn the reader that Nicola Barker (henceforth referred to as The Author) has been granted **absolutely no access** to the thoughts and feel-ings of the character Gyasi 'Chance' Ebo (henceforth referred to as The Subject). At his inception, The Subject seemed not only a willing, but an **actively enthusiastic** parti-cipant in the project, yet after several weeks of engagement became increasingly cynical and uncooperative, to the point of threatening to withdraw from the enterprise altogether if The Author deigned to encroach, unduly, upon his 'interior life'.*

For this reason, where possible, The Author has attempted (with The Subject's permission) to side-step his wanton opacity by 'calmly theorising' on The Subject's possible feel-ings/thoughts/motivations and then transcribing these ideas into the text using an <u>entirely different font</u> (the standard font is Baskerville. The Subject has requested AMERICAN TYPEWRITER *as an alternative for the chapters in which he is to be heavily featured.* AMERICAN

149

TYPEWRITER *was agreed upon after lengthy consultations with The Subject. The Author should make it plain that* AMERICAN TYPEWRITER *is a font that does not permit the use of italicisation, something that she worries — in the light of her ebullient 'style' — may ultimately be inhibiting to the feel and flow of I Am Sovereign. If this is indeed the case, The Author apologises — again — unreservedly).*

It would be difficult — nay foolish — for The Author to speculate at this juncture on the whys and the wherefores of The Subject's taciturnity. The Author is both saddened and frustrated by The Subject's seeming unwillingness to place his trust/confidence in her (The Author's) natural sense of balance and fair play in relation to this/her text(s). The Author has informed The Subject — via telepathy and WhatsApp — that she is merely trying to tell the simple — almost trite — story of a twenty-odd-minute house viewing in Llandudno during which The Subject makes a brief, relatively inconsequential appearance, but The Subject — while accepting that he was conceived of as 'present' during said viewing — is determined to remain abstruse, impenetrable and enigmatic. The Subject also disagrees with the idea that his appearance is merely 'inconsequential', but rather describes his role as 'climactic', even 'seminal' (The Author is unconvinced that The Subject understands the real meaning of the word 'seminal').

The Author wishes The Reader to understand that she thought — long and hard — about cutting The Subject from I Am Sovereign altogether, but ultimately felt that to do so would involve a profound compromise of her febrile and unconstrained imagination (The Subject is unconvinced that The Author understands the real meaning of the word 'febrile').

The Author sincerely hopes that The Reader will extend a measure of compassion and understanding towards herself/ the text during the following three chapters and do their best to work with The Author in imagining the extraordinary richness and diversity of The Subject's potential role — as it was originally conceived — in I Am Sovereign.

(The Subject also sincerely hopes that The Reader will extend a measure of compassion and understanding towards himself/his right to self-determination during the following three chapters and do their best to work with him in imagining the extraordinary richness and diversity of his actual role — as opposed to the role he is to be patronisingly 'gifted' by The Author — in I Am Sovereign.)

The Author wishes to make it clear (and she feels that this actually 'goes without saying' — although she is saying it) that it has been necessary to make certain — very subtle — adjustments to I Am Sovereign in order to try and counterbalance the problems engendered by The Subject's unexpected reticence. Novels are finely honed and delicate organisms. The character of Wang Shu (for example) has been greatly reduced and simplified as a consequence of these necessary adjustments. In the original version Wang Shu spent only a fraction of her time on the phone talking in Chinese. Several pages in which Wang Shu spoke – most touchingly and evocatively – about her skill in playing the 'erhu', a traditional two ('er' in Chinese) stringed instrument with its horsetail and bamboo bow and box-like body featuring – among other exotica: python skin – were summarily eradicated. These included the moving story of Wang Shu's unsuccessful (nay, borderline tragic), audition for the Guangzhou Symphony Youth Orchestra as a teenager, her shows of extraordinary bravery and persistence in bouncing back from this terrible disappointment, and her eventual – joyous/life-affirming – acceptance into the National Youth Orchestra of China.

In some senses these scenes represented an exquisite (and all the more so for being both utterly unexpected and immensely well-judged) 'opening up' of Wang Shu, and The Author sincerely considered them to be among some of the finest work she has ever produced.

(The Subject would not agree with this particular 'value-judgement'.)

The character of Morpheus was added to I Am Sovereign in the final draft. In the earlier version a kitten called Sindy featured, but this kitten was a tortoiseshell longhair and The Subject became irritated by the way her fur kept marking his white jeans and compromising his 'look' (even though Charles kindly supplied him with a selection of lint rollers throughout the writing of I Am Sovereign's first draft).

(The Subject would like it to be known that The Author insisted on his wearing white jeans when in fact he had pre-ferred to wear grey, moleskin jodhpurs.)

Finally, it should be noted that in the original version of I Am Sovereign the character of Avigail at no point vacates the property on Ty Isa Road. Due to her high levels of profes-sionalism, the character, Avigail, would never willingly leave clients in the lurch while showing a vendor's home. To do so would <u>run counter to her very nature</u>.

(The Subject finds it 'frankly laughable' that Avigail's professionalism should be mentioned in this context. He has no idea what relevance Avigail's professionalism – or want of professionalism – has to do with the issue at hand.)

153

In some senses The Author considers it 'little short of a tragedy' that The Subject's decisions have impacted so heavily on I Am Sovereign as a whole, but strenuously maintains that she respects his choices and – ultimately – bears The Subject no lasting ill will.

(The Subject calls this final statement by The Author 'sentimental, sententious poppycock'.)

7.

IF YOU BELIEVE IN TELEKINESIS, PLEASE RAISE MY HAND

While Gyasi 'Chance' Ebo *is* extremely intelligent, he has no way of knowing that Charles is running scared of the bailiffs. Lucky for Gyasi, though, Charles announces this fact as soon as he discovers Gyasi (up to his knees in kapok and rifling through large piles of teddy-related detritus) in his sewing room.

Charles all but bellows: 'This is forced entry! Which creditor are you here for? What have you taken control of? I demand to see documentation!'

'The door was open, my friend,' Gyasi responds coolly, with a shrug.

The sewing room is very small – it's really just a large cupboard which an optimist trying to sell Charles's house might call 'an office'. Charles is a tall man but he is extremely good at compressing himself into small spaces when needs must. And

Charles is very sensitive to the idea of work/life balance and therefore refuses, on principle, to allow his work to take up too much space (either literally or metaphorically).

Charles has no intention of becoming a workaholic. He's way too complacent and savvy for that.

Bear making is 'just a job'. It's not 'a calling'. It's not 'a drive'. It's not 'a passion'.

Gyasi 'Chance' Ebo is magnificently slender. He is exactly six feet tall.

(*The Subject is six feet one inch tall.*)

He dresses in an elegantly feminine manner.

(*The Subject finds this analysis 'patronising in the extreme'.*)

Not as a woman, but as a fine-boned man who enjoys wearing feminine-style clothes (tight, white jeans, pretty, pastel-coloured shirts, a bright yellow mackintosh, cinched at the waist with a little belt).

(*The Subject finds the above description 'odd – disquieting, even borderline disturbing'.*)

He is a pretty boy.

(*The Subject says, 'What?! Does she seriously expect to get away with this?!'*)

He has knock-off designer sunglasses pushed up on his head.

(*The Subject's Tom Ford 'Dimitry' TF334 [£181.33] sunglasses were purchased at the Cardiff branch of John Lewis – 2-/0-/2018 – with a gift card on the occasion of his birthday. He has all the relevant documentation to prove it.*

The date has been partially obscured to avoid identity theft.

The Subject wishes it to be known that he laughed – out loud – at the rich irony of the above statement.)

He is sporting a pair of lemon-coloured loafers. His eyebrows are nothing short of sublime.

(*The Subject insists that he has never groomed or plucked his eyebrows – or managed them in any way – and that the above sentence represents a personal slur 'cleverly couched in the language of a compliment'.*)

No. *No*. This is ridiculous. It simply isn't workable. Not only am I incredibly tense re the (possible, future) want of italics and the potential horror of AMERICAN TYPEWRITER undermining the calm fluidity of the text, but Gyasi 'Chance' Ebo's perpetual interruptions (in smug legalese) and his hectoring, self-righteous tone are completely intolerable. Everything is contested. Everything is contrary.

And I need full access. I demand it! *Why* this sudden reticence on Gyasi's part? What does it mean? Why can't he just pull his head in and comply – roll up his sleeves and muck in – like everybody else? Wang Shu is grumpy – lumpen – self-determined – hard-boiled – borderline obnoxious – but *even she* has been a dream to work with by comparison (yes, always on the phone to her Chinese agent complaining about the number of words she and Ying Yue have in the text as a whole, but generally very open – very good-natured).

It's the pervasive atmosphere of ill will seeping into every line that I'm really struggling with. And I find myself over-compensating – over-thinking – being excessively complimentary and sycophantic – granting Gyasi favours that none of the other characters get (he has lovely eyebrows, sure, but do I really need to make 'a thing' out of them? And this ludicrous middle name 'Chance' which he insists upon because it helps to identify his page on Instagram). I'm nervous around him! I'm tentative, which (I firmly believe) is severely deleterious to the free-spirited atmosphere that my unconscious mind/muse/*blah* demands as a prerequisite to true, unencumbered creativity.

Enough is enough.

I am henceforth kicking Gyasi 'Chance' Ebo out of the novella (as I type this I notice – with a slight smirk – how spellcheck repeatedly changes Gyasi's surname from Ebo to Ego. That can't be a coincidence, can it?).

Although … hmm … Although … might it be *good* for me (for my wayward spirit) to try and be a little bit more considered – a little bit more careful – in general? Doesn't Richard Grannon often say that the urge to 'naive innocence' is a neurotic one? Is my urge to create uninhibitedly a neurotic one, therefore?

Shouldn't a person's Inner Child (cf. *I'm OK – You're OK*) be gently curbed by their Inner Adult on the odd occasion?

When I consider how obliging the other characters have been ... I mean Charles has been incredibly
helpful. He didn't turn a hair when I exaggerated his
'collections' into wholesale hoarding. He accepted
that it worked as a kind of extended metaphor in
the text. And he hates the name Charles but accepts
that it's suitably bland and uncontentious with a
'royal'/'sovereign' undertow.

I am Sovereign.

I *am* Sovereign!

I am Sovereign.
I am Queen of my own serenity.

Yes.

     peaceful entry

(Sorry – this is just a note I left on the page to remind
myself of something else.)

Abigail (who is now Jewish, and called A*v*igail,
although Charles keeps forgetting this and calling

her A*b*igail, which has my poor copy-editor, Morag, literally pulling her hair out) is tremendously obliging. And this runs counter to her character, which is fractious, at best.

Ying Yue? Who can tell with Ying Yue? Who knows what Ying Yue will do next? Although there was an interesting sub-plot with her brother – Fei Hung – which she suddenly went cold on and I suspect this was Gyasi's malign influence. I'm not certain what it entailed, but I think it involved Fei Hung getting a graduate student pregnant during his time studying Business Law at the University of Bangor.

Huh.

'Golden Child'.

And Wang Shu is still none the wiser.

I am going back to Chapter 2. It will take me literally a couple of lines to rework the whole thing ...

So, from page 57, two paras down.

'There's a small issue with the bailiff,' Charles explains, ignoring this.

As they walk up the road and approach Charles's house they stroll past a tiny, elderly man who is wearing a giant pair of dark glasses and holding a white cane. He is standing next to a large, blue, waste disposal bin. He is perfectly still.

The blind old man is illumined.

I have actually changed the font into **AMERICAN TYPEWRITER** as a gentle 'screw you' to Gyasi 'Chance' Ego – E*bo*
E*bo* E*bo*.

The revised version runs:

'*There's a small issue with the bailiff,' Charles explains, ignoring this.*
As they walk up the road and approach Charles's house they stroll past a handsome, dark-skinned, willowy youth who is leaning, nonchalantly, against a large, blue waste disposal bin. Avigail's eyes return to him, several times, slightly perplexed, to peruse his pretty, yellow raincoat (there is no sign of rain).

This yellow raincoat man is illumined.

I don't think it works so well. Begs more questions. But what the heck. It'll do.

Then Chapter 6. Second from last page, first paragraph:

Well, whatever the story Charles is living now about this situation –

Poltergeist?

– it is 99.9 per cent unlikely that his story (creative as he undoubtedly is, inventive as he undoubtedly is) involves a fiercely intelligent, immaculately attired, twenty-three-year-old Ethiopian professional carer called Gyasi 'Chance' Ebo riffling furiously though his teddy bear collection.

Now changed to:

Well, **whatever** *the story Charles is living now about this situation —*

Poltergeist?

— it is 99.9 per cent unlikely that his story (creative as he undoubtedly is, inventive as he undoubtedly is) involves an incredibly persistent, highly intelligent, terrifyingly indignant, partially sighted seventy-eight-year-old man of diminutive stature called Denny Neale (wearing filthy, green dungarees with a neatly plaited Robert Crumb's Mr Natural-style beard and a giant magnifying glass) riffling furiously though his teddy bear collection.

Actually, I think this works better.

Overcompensating with too many descriptive words, though.

Screw Gyasi 'Chance' Ebo.

Need to bring Denny Neale completely *TO LIFE*!

Ka-pow!

7. (revised)

IF YOU BELIEVE IN TELEKINESIS, PLEASE RAISE MY HAND

While Denny Neale *is* extremely intelligent, he has no way of knowing that Charles is running scared of the bailiffs. Lucky for Denny, though, Charles announces this fact as soon as he discovers him (up to his knees in kapok and rifling carelessly through large piles of teddy-related detritus) in his sewing room.

Charles all but bellows: 'This is forced entry! Which creditor are you here for? What have you taken control of? I demand to see documentation!'

'The door was open,' Denny responds with a shrug, waving his giant magnifying glass at Charles, almost airily. 'This is peaceful access.'

Denny has a rare, inherited vision disorder called Achromatopsia which means that he cannot see colour and is unbelievably sensitive to bright light (in certain circumstances this often renders him all but blind).

The sewing room is very small – it's really just a large cupboard which an optimist trying to sell Charles's house might call 'an office'. Charles is a tall man but he is extremely good at compressing himself into small spaces when needs must. He is also highly attuned to the idea of work/life balance and therefore refuses to let his work take up too much space (literally or metaphorically).

Charles has no intention of becoming a workaholic. He's way too complacent and savvy for that.

Bear making is 'just a job'. It's not 'a calling'. It's not 'a drive'. It's not 'a passion'.

Charles continues to charge forward as Denny speaks and is now standing in the sewing room alongside Denny. He is towering above Denny. There is very little room in the sewing room, so 'normal' ideas connected to 'acceptable notions of personal space' cannot apply here. Charles is quickly joined in the sewing room by Avigail who feels a (possibly excessive) sense of responsibility with regard to people currently occupying/inhabiting Charles's home (even Charles himself is included in this schema. Certainly Morpheus).

'What's going on?' she demands. Avigail also towers over Denny Neale who stands at four feet seven inches in his socks (he is currently wearing a pair of plain black plimsolls with thin rubber soles – the kind you'd wear in school PE classes. He treasures the notion of pliability).

Denny Neale likes women and so takes the opportunity to hold his giant magnifying glass up into Avigail's face to scrutinise her.

'Who are you?' he asks. 'The wife?'

'Don't be ridiculous!' Charles snorts.

'Who are *you*?' Denny asks, moving the giant magnifying glass across to Charles.

'I'm Charles!' Charles says.

Charles is currently feeling:

Indignant.

'Charles is the vendor,' Avigail adds (as if Charles's identity must always henceforth be closely bound up with his selling of a property).

'What does your T-shirt say?' Denny asks. Denny is eye-level with the slogan on Charles's T-shirt. He applies his magnifying glass to Charles's T-shirt.

Charles refuses to tell Denny what his T-shirt says. Why *should* he tell this tiny, odd, invasive old man in dark glasses what his T-shirt says?

As if reading Charles's thoughts Denny adds, 'I am legally blind.'

He is still holding up his giant magnifying glass to Charles's chest and trying to read the slogan on his T-shirt but its meaning eludes him.

Denny smells – very strongly – of quince (although Charles does not know what quinces smell like. Charles has never encountered a quince. Or if Charles *has* encountered a quince, then he hasn't been aware of the fact that it *is* a quince. Quinces are basically an unknown quantity to Charles).

'Are you wearing Britney Spears's Fantasy?' Avigail wonders, sniffing.

Avigail is scent-savvy.

Avigail has a great nose.

Charles frowns at Avigail. He has no idea what the hell Avigail is talking about.

Charles is currently feeling:

Mystified.
Indignant.
Irritated.
Invaded.
Wrong-footed.

'Quince.' Denny nods. 'I make a special perfume from quinces by steeping the fruit in oil. Then I rub it on to my beard. Sometimes, at season's change, I rub it on to my feet and on to my hands. Oh. And on to my elbows and on to my testicles.'

Charles is struggling to work out why a legally blind man (smelling very strongly of quinces – *or so he says* ... Charles has no particular incentive to trust this man who has, after all, just broken into his home) would be working as a bailiff in North Wales.

'I've been told before that Fantasy has a strong whiff of quince to it,' Denny adds. 'The other quince-heavy one is by Chanel – Chance Eau Tendre – but the Roman name that the scent is traditionally known by – although the Arabs used it, and the Greeks – is Melinum. It's very comforting, very warm – somewhere between a pear and an apple.'

169

'It's an amazingly evocative scent.' Avigail nods, remarking to herself on how many clauses there are in Denny Neale's sentences (although she doesn't actually know that this tiny man is called 'Denny Neale'). Generally, Avigail finds, when someone you've only recently become acquainted with speaks in this particular fashion they are either incredibly interesting or intensely boring. Because they are so confident. And considered. They colonise space (air, the human/social geography) with language.

Just following these thoughts (in addendum – drawing up behind the thoughts with a dramatic skidding of brakes) is the word 'testicles'.

The after-shock of this word hangs in the air between them, vibrating. And there are exclamation marks. Plenty of them. Invisible to the human eye. Yet palpable.

Testicles?

!!!!!!!!!!!

'I once ate a quince jam – a kind of jelly or ... I don't know ... *paste* while on holiday in Spain,' Avigail says ...

Testicles?

'They serve it with cheese.'
'Membrillo.' Denny nods. 'You bake the quinces and then sieve them, set it in trays ...'

Quince oil *on his testicles*?

It would be fair to say that Denny is something of an authority on quinces.
Charles imagines Denny wearing a T-shirt that reads: I AM AN AUTHORITY ON QUINCES.

Charles didn't register the comment about testicles because he was too busy asking himself how he was feeling:

Claustrophobic.
Bemused.
Focused.
Unfocused.

But are 'focused' and 'unfocused' feelings, as such?

No.

Not feelings. Yet they are certainly 'felt'.

Not feelings, as such.

So what are they?

States?

Hmm. What would the score in Scrabble be for the word 'quince'? Charles wonders.
Off the cuff he guesstimates 18 – which isn't a bad score.

Although 'guesstimates' is probably around 14.
Although it probably wouldn't be allowed.
Although words are words and exist and flourish and gain in plausibility simply by dint of being used.
Words are promiscuous, by nature.

Even so.

As he ponders Charles has a nagging feeling that there's something he should be getting to grips with. Oh yes. This tiny man with the magnifying glass has broken into his home and is taking an itinerary of all his possessions in the hope of relieving him of them in the short to medium term.

Testicles?

Having said that, Denny Neale (although Charles has no idea what this little man is called) isn't carrying a clipboard with him, or pen (attached with a bit of string to the clipboard) for the making of lists etc. Although he has professed to being legally blind so a clipboard would be of limited use to him, surely? Even with a giant magnifying glass? Charles finds himself at once impressed and appalled that Llandudno Council have seen fit to employ this man. Perhaps his blindness is a recent thing?

Um ...

Testicles?

'Have you been blind for long?' Charles asks.
Charles actually interrupts a conversation between Abigail

AV-IGAIL, CHARLES!

AV-IGAIL!
AV-IGAIL!
AV-IGAIL!
AV-IGAIL!
AV-IGAIL!

Morag doesn't get paid for correcting *every*, tiny mistake, Charles. Morag gets paid for copy-editing *the entire book*. Morag already wasted several precious hours yesterday afternoon checking the lyrics to that ridiculous song about China that Ying Yue sang in the last chapter and is currently feeling pretty pissed off. So you are really wearing her down by doing this. Just get it into your thick head already:

AV-IGAIL!

AV-IGAIL!

Yes.

Good enough is more than enough. For me.

But not for a copy-editor.

And certainly not for a high-grade copy-editor, like Morag.

Good enough is *not* enough. For a high-grade copy-editor, like Morag.

'... a special kind of blue cheese ...' Avigail is saying.

Fucking hell! Avigail inhales, sharply, mid-sentence. Did Charles just ask a virtual stranger how long he has been blind for? Did he *seriously* just do that? What kind of a ...?
What kind of a social retard *is* he?! A fifty-year-old man! Behaving like a twelve-year-old boy!
(Charles is actually a forty-year-old man behaving like a nine-year-old boy.)

Ying Yue suddenly enters the room. Ying Yue runs into the room. She's just very anxious not to get left behind. Although the room is already full to capacity so she's more like a line-backer charging, aggressively, into a scrum, than a normal, bounda-ried human being.

Ying Yue tends to be immensely vague for extended intervals (and there's no pattern to this behaviour – it seems essentially random and erratic) but then to overcompensate (or make recompense – although *to whom* exactly it is uncertain, even to Ying Yue) by a brief spate of intense hyperactivity. She will (for example) stand staring at herself, blankly, in the bathroom mirror for entire minutes on end, and then suddenly start brushing her hair with demented levels of ferocity.

Brush!
Brush!Brush!Brush!Brush!Brush!Brush!Brush!Brush!Brush!
Brush!Brush!Brush!Brush!Brush!Brush!Brush!Brush!Brush!
Brush!

Then more stillness.

No rhyme or reason.

Then a sigh.

Then
Brush!Brush!Brush!Brush!Brush!Brush!Brush!Brush!Brush!
Brush!Brush!Brush!Brush!Brush!Brush!Brush!

So far as she is aware, Ying Yue is still on a house viewing. Ying Yue is slightly confused by the fact that Avigail
and Charles have disappeared from the kitchen at
high speed. So she follows them – after some inten-
sive scrutiny of a cracked floor tile – also at speed.

She is conforming ... although a certain amount of
time has passed in between. But this is of no significance to Ying Yue. Time is something inessential
– redundant, cosmetic – to Ying Yue.

And she is breaking away from Wang Shu (who
is talking on the phone in Chinese) so she needs
to move quickly in order to smash through Wang
Shu's powerful force-field. Like a tiny rocket defy-
ing the pull of gravity.

When Ying Yue sees Denny Neale she simply
presumes that he is another client of Avigail's who
has turned up early for his own viewing of Charles's
property.

Yes.

Either that or he is Charles's father.

Yes.

Denny Neale looks like Charles's father.

Denny Neale is small (unlike Charles) but he does
breathe and have two hands and two eyes, like

Charles. Although not like Charles because Charles is different. Very different.

Father and son are very, very different.
It is almost a miracle that these two individuals hail from the same gene-pool.
Life is extraordinary!!

'World is crazier than we know it,' etc.!

Ying Yue is very big on first impressions. Ying Yue actually finds it difficult to move away from her first impressions. First impressions are gut led. They are raw. They are natural. They are instinctive. They are deep. And Ying Yue lives by them. So Denny Neale (although Ying Yue does not know that this little blind old man with quince-oiled testicles *is* Denny Neale) will now always be Charles's father AND Avigail's other client (therefore a rival) at one and the same time in Ying Yue's mind, even though these two notions are, at some level, mutually exclusive . . .

When Ying Yue and Charles marry (approximately a year on from this house viewing), Ying Yue will feel a slight pang of anxiety that Denny Neale is not present at the ceremony (which will be held, at Wang Shu's insistence, on the end of Llandudno's remarkably long pier), and as Charles pushes the ring on to Ying Yue's finger, she will wonder, idly, whether Charles's father (Denny Neale) ever managed to find a nice house for himself.

And she will think, almost wistfully, of quinces.

But it would be a shame to spoil the present moment by glancing, casually (head tilted, almost squinting), into the future.

Ying Yue has such a marvellous, generous, *porous* mind. Let that – and that alone – suffice for now.

Hmm.

But why would Charles's father be trying to buy Charles's mother's old house from Charles (with Avigail's assistance)? Unless Avigail was, in fact, Charles's sister?

His long-lost sister?

Does that work?

Yes!
Of course it works!
Of course it does!

Oh my goodness – this is a very small room!
It's like being crammed into a tiny elevator!

Hardly any space at all!

And ...

Oooh!
Oooh! *Teddies!* Look! *Teddies!!*

Everywhere!

Teddies!

Just like in heaven which is ONLY teddies! Oh! Yes! And tiny squirrels with little silver wings and angel-faces! And dragons who breathe bubbles not flames!

Ying Yue's own sweet face is now wreathed in smiles.

She bounces up and down with uncontrollable excitement.

Lots and lots and lots and lots!

Teddies!
Teddies!
Teddy-love!
Love-teddy!

Oh!
Oh!
Oh!
Oh!

Ying Yue grabs an utterly bemused Charles and – still bouncing up and down – hugs him, violently.

YING YUE SOOOO HAPPY NOW!!

8.

LET'S EAT GRANDMA.
LET'S EAT, GRANDMA.
COMMAS SAVE LIVES.

Yes, Wang Shu *is* always on the phone talking in Chinese, but it would be deeply misguided to automatically glean from this fact that she is – in some crass and unimaginative way – 'avoiding life', or 'never quite in the moment', or 'simply bloody rude', etc.
Oh no. Far from it.
Richard Grannon may well call this too-easy, knee-jerk-y response a 'faulty perception'.

Wang Shu is indubitably somewhat rude and distracted and self-involved, but she is actually often having *quite interesting* conversations on the phone in Chinese. Relatively *important* conversations on the phone in Chinese.

During the course of this brief, twenty-odd-minute house viewing (for example), Wang Shu has organised a visa via her over-worked London 'arranger' for a trip she is planning to Bolivia in the spring to try and finally bring about an atmosphere of concord between Bolivia and Chile after the many decades of rancour that have been generated over Bolivia's loss of sea access (it was actually taken away between the years of 1879 and 1883. And there have been no diplomatic relations since 1978). Yes. It's a long, interesting and ultimately rather tragic story. But we don't really have time to go into it here.

There simply isn't room. This is just a novella (approx. 23,000 words +).

Wang Shu has also come up with an interesting recipe which produces a variant of tofu out of water chestnuts. Wang Shu (and her sponsors) firmly believe that this new foodstuff will revolutionise Western vegetarian cuisine (although the prototype currently contains goose fat).

As she was talking on the phone in Chinese by the front door (early on in the viewing) Wang Shu was actually telling her business partner, Li Qiang (and in no uncertain terms, either), 'You *can't* replace the goose fat! The goose fat is key! Every inch of fucking flavour is *contained* in the goose fat you big *shagua*!'*

*shagua means, quite literally, 'dumb melon'.

Wang Shu invested £17,000 sterling shortly after she first entered Charles's kitchen in a small, independent Chinese film provisionally entitled *Blue Shadows* (*Lan se Yinying*) about a woman's passion for her water buffalo. The water buffalo is rescued from a fighting circuit. The woman is a talented calligrapher. The calligraphic sign for water buffalo is very pretty and plain in Chinese: a kind of double K followed by a kind of double T. Obviously there is much more to the plot of *Blue Shadows* than this (an alcoholic father who manufactures exceptional calligraphy brushes out of wolf hair being just one strand), but little will actually be served by describing its various twists and turns in detail here.

Sorry about that.

Even as I type Wang Shu is telling a bossy, well-educated Chinese girl currently occupying a private birthing room at a hospital in Bangor that a recently delivered baby is a bastard. And no, Fei Hung will *not* undertake a paternity test.

Forget it.

Get lost.

Had de?

(Okay? In Chinese.)

Lan fu!

(Slut! In Chinese.)

In thirty seconds' time, Wang Shu will initiate a deal with Charles's main creditor in regard to the house. She will make a daring cash offer of 20 per cent under its estimated market price. This offer will be impossible for Charles/his creditors to resist.

Wang Shu supposes the place will make a perfectly good home for Ying Yue and that over-sized, over-sensitive, patently deranged finger-tapping chump once they are wed.

Wang Shu has been paying scant attention to either Ying Yue *or* Charles over the past seventeen minutes, but she has, nonetheless, detected CHEMISTRY between them.

186

Wang Shu is actually one of the most horribly subtle unsubtle people who has ever walked the earth.

Wang Shu is actually one of the most horribly sensitive insensitive people who has ever walked the earth.

Wang Shu is actually one of the most horribly intuitive . . .

etc.

(no, that last one doesn't quite work).

Because:

Good enough is *always* enough. For Wang Shu.

Wang Shu has not even seen the bedrooms, yet, but she espied the teddy bears while walking through to the kitchen and firing the accountant currently in charge of overseeing an extremely lucrative export business that she has run for the past twelve years shipping Heinz Baked Beans, Heinz Salad Cream and Heinz Mushroom Soup to the burgeoning Chinese market in Shanghai.

On the phone.

In Chinese.

Hmm.

Charles has skills. And Wang Shu – who can smell class a mile off, principally because she has very little of it herself, and very little *need* of it herself, in fact despises it, for the most part – is the woman best served to exploit those skills of his.

Yikes.

Although this will probably be good for Charles, in the long run.

Although the above sentence is entirely predicated on what 'good for Charles' actually means. The phrase is relative.

'Good for Charles' from Wang Shu's perspective. Not necessarily 'good for Charles' from Charles's perspective.

Charles doesn't really know what's 'good for him', though. Some things Charles *thinks* are good for him aren't good for him at all. And some things that Wang Shu thinks are 'good for him' won't be good for him, either.

If only Richard Grannon were here to sort this stuff out.

But he isn't here (he can't be), because at this precise moment in time he is probably addressing a symposium in Latvia on narcissistic abuse, or standing – breathing deeply – on a pristine beach in Ibiza and posting a photo of it on Instagram to his ten zillion followers before being interviewed by an improbably attractive brunette on a local news programme in Spanish.

Richard Grannon doesn't think that people are simply entitled to be happy. But he does think that people are entitled to fight (tooth and claw) to live their happiest, their most productive and their most authentic lives.

To be Sovereign.
To be present, positive and boundaried.

The happiest people are generally those who are willing to be flexible.
And to compromise.

Richard Grannon says that you need to 'kick the legs out from under negative beliefs by dint of critical thinking'.

It's all about taking a quick step back, drawing a deep breath, and gently telling yourself, 'Okay, so this *feels* pretty bad as things currently stand, but why not take a moment to try and focus on what is actually *right* about this situation?'

Of course this is just so much hot air to Wang Shu who doesn't really have time to think about how she is feeling or how anyone else is feeling, least of all Charles.

Wang Shu likes a man who can do his own washing, though.

And Charles is tidy. A tidy hoarder.

Although in actual fact Charles isn't really a hoarder, but is simply a hoarder for the benefit of this narrative.

Okay. Don't freak out.

He really *is* a hoarder.

Honest.

Charles hoards.

He has been hoarding his feelings, too. Storing them away in giant, impermeable vats and never actually feeling them.

Poor Charles.

Charles needs to prise open the cardboard box of his emotions (or the impermeable vat of his emotions — you choose) and check out what's inside.

Ouch!
Feel it.
Writhe around for a while, sobbing, plaintively.
Punch the walls.
Then repair the walls (because Wang Shu now owns the house and he doesn't want to incur her formidable wrath).
Then pick himself up, dust himself down and get on with LIVING HIS BEST LIFE.
Same as everybody else.
Yeah.
Put all those pesky feelings to good use.

Because if you won't let yourself feel the bad stuff, you automatically lose the ability to experience the good.

You become zombie-fied.

Tap, tap, tap ...

I am king of my own ...

Charles is currently feeling:

Absolutely fucking terrified.

Let. Me. Get. The. Hell. Out. Of. Here.

Avigail has a fair idea, though (a fair idea of what might be 'good for Charles'). Avigail would be able to summarise her extensive theories on this matter in approximately six, long, heavily claused sentences (*à la* Denny Neale). One of those sentences would definitely contain the colloquial phrase 'a good kick up the arse'.

And Ying Yue?

What does Ying Yue think might be 'good for Charles'?

That would be hard to say.

Ying Yue thinks Teflon is a variety of apple, after all.

Although in an alternate universe Teflon may actually *be* a variety of apple.

And commas may seriously *endanger* lives.

Uh-huh.

Think: tiny, (*Ka-boom!*) grammatical hand grenades.

9.

PROCRASTINATORS UNITE!

Denny Neale actually has a teddy bear stuffed down the back of his dungarees. It is *his* teddy bear (um … morally speaking). It belongs to *him* (um … ethically speaking). It has been paid for, in advance. It is a teddy bear that he – Denny Neale – commissioned from Charles over eighteen months ago and Charles has refused to part with it, even though Denny Neale has sent him a succession of pleading letters/emails (and some threatening letters/ emails), none of which has Charles read because Charles is officially In Hiding From Reality.

The teddy bear in question is dressed like a goth. Its beautiful, little costume has been fashioned (by Charles) from an old, *Damned* T-shirt and a pair of black German-issue military combats once owned and worn by Denny Neale's former lover/partner Samson Horny (this was not his given name) who worked for many years as a second-hand CD seller in the thriving coastal town of Abersoch on the Llyn Peninsula.

'Excuse me,' Avigail suddenly interrupts.
(As it happens, nobody is currently speaking, since Ying Yue is still hugging Charles – while bouncing – and Charles is still feeling complete astonishment at *being* hugged –

Yes. Charles is feeling:

Astonished.
Delighted.
Mortified.
Invaded.
Overwhelmed.

Ridiculous.

and Denny Neale isn't currently speaking either – he is choosing not to answer Charles's slightly clumsy question about how long he has been blind for, remember? – because he is presently too pre-occupied with debating how the heck he is going to get out of this stupidly tiny room which is now stuffed with three other people; and can't he hear yet another – a fourth person? – talking loudly in Chinese in some distant corner of the house?)

'Excuse me,' Avigail repeats, 'but would you mind telling me what actually became of the oyster shell?'

This question appears to be addressed to Ying Yue.

It would be difficult to know why Avigail has chosen this precise moment to re-open the whole 'oyster-shell-strike/non-strike farrago'.

Hmm.
What is the story that Avigail is living now about this situation?

Or – perhaps more pertinently – what is the story that *we* are living now about what Avigail is living now about this situation?

Is it Avigail's Toxic Super-Ego suddenly declaring war on her newly-blissed-out/faith-infused Adult/ Inner Child?

Is Avigail feeling weird (and – quite frankly – inex-plicable) pangs of jealousy due to the sudden bond being forged between Ying Yue and Charles? Is her apparent antipathy to Charles actually a subconscious rejection of a *surreptitious unconscious attraction* to Charles?

Is Avigail simply displacing the social/emotional anxiety (recently generated by Denny Neale suddenly/randomly using the word 'testicles') by reverting her attention back to another socially/emotionally contested incident from earlier on in the viewing?

Yes.
All of the above.

No.
None of the above.

Actually, both.

Yes, both. At the same time.

Because people are, by their very nature, contradictory.
Because people are, by their very nature, paradoxical.

Aside from Wang Shu, that is.

Wang Shu is terrifyingly single-minded.
Wang Shu is possessed of an almost supernatural coherence.

But *where* is the oyster shell?
Huh?
Was there actually an oyster shell?
Huh?
Is Ying Yue currently in possession of said oyster shell?
Huh?

Gyasi 'Chance' Ebo actually researched online (when he was still featured in the novella – although not while 'on page', but while 'off-page') and discovered that seagulls *do* habitually drop oysters from great heights to smash them and devour their innards, but very rarely – if ever – do they carry them beyond the confines of the beach to do so. Gyasi 'Chance' Ebo shared this information via Snapchat with a group of his friends, none of whom have had the chance to read the novel *I Am Sovereign* yet (and none of whom have been invented by The Author yet) because the book is still actually being written (this will be difficult for The Reader to understand, as they hold a perfect copy in their hand, but it makes perfect sense to The Author as she types this sentence, so The Reader will just have to suspend judgement and go with it) and – let's face it – Gyasi 'Chance' Ebo is a relatively insignificant character in *I Am Sovereign* who has now been virtually expunged from the narrative by The Author.

Damn him.

Damn Gyasi 'Chance' Ebo and his fatuous interruptions.
Damn Gyasi 'Chance' Ebo and his persistent thrusting for narrative significance/insignificance.

The Author knows FOR A FACT that Gyasi 'Chance' Ebo's glasses are knock-off Burberry Doodle Square Frame Sunglasses, not Tom Ford Dimitrys, as stated earlier in the text.

The Author has also (only recently) come across the sentence:
'What are the stories, the fictions, from which you derive your sense of self?' in Eckhart Tolle's *Stillness Speaks* and thinks that *this* may actually be the

original source of Richard Grannon's sister's yoga teacher's phrase.

Unless Eckhart Tolle actually derived this phrase from Richard Grannon's sister's yoga teacher, that is.
Who's to say?

Everything's up for grabs, here.

The Author is also thinking about re-writing the chapter about Avigail and silence (Chapter 5) because she is now wondering whether *stillness* is inherently more interesting (conceptually/spiritually) than silence, and more rarely addressed – as a subject – by other writers.

It's so *wearying* when everything is being perpetually challenged and contested like this, though, isn't it?
But shouldn't fiction strive to echo life (where everything is constantly being challenged and contested)?
Or is fiction merely a soothing balm, a soft breeze, a quiet confirmation, a temporary release?

Why should it be either/or?

Can't fiction be exquisitely paradoxical?

But then which of us goes to Dreams or IKEA to buy a new mattress and then takes the thing home and carefully peels back the strong, clean fabric that neatly covers it to reveal the springs?

We don't. We just bounce on to the mattress, stretch out, sigh, and fall blissfully asleep.

The Author suspects that this novella (which is currently in danger of becoming a novel so needs to end quite soon) is either extremely deep or unbelievably trite.
It's impossible to tell.
The Author (Gyasi 'Chance' Ebo claims) will persist in calling it 'unbelievably trite' because she is fundamentally disingenuous.
The Author (The Author claims) will persist in calling it 'unbelievably trite' because – at some profound level – it *is* unbelievably trite.

Nothing of much note happens, really, does it?

Aside from the oyster shell strike?

Everything else is merely filler and back story.

And a certain amount of waffling on about Richard Grannon whose work The Author greatly admires (and who has recently closed down his Instagram account and declared war on the word 'narcissist'), and Lucy Molloy, who The Author enjoys watching on YouTube. Lucy Molloy gave birth to a baby (Hendrix) a short while ago. This development has filled her life with an immense joy and a renewed purpose, which, to be perfectly honest, is slightly irritating for The Author in terms of the narrative/ moral/social commentary The Author is surreptitiously asserting. Or not actually asserting but kind of asserting.

The Author is recently returned from a trip to Normandy, in France, which she undertook with a friend – also called Nicola – who owns a farmhouse there and happens to be one of the world's leading experts on the vulva. The Author wrote much of Chapter 7 while sitting on the grass in the other Nicola's paddock under a giant oak tree with acorns falling down all around her. On the final day of her trip, the other Nicola mentioned, in passing, that sitting in long grass may have placed The Author in danger of being attacked by a local burrowing insect which lives in the long grass in that particular region of France. Said insect burrows stealthily into the body's warm folds and crevices and generates an almost unspeakable level of itching. There is no known treatment for this itching. Although – on a positive note – the parasite can only unleash its itch on a single occasion. After falling prey to its wiles the first time, the victim will then become immune.

The Author naturally asked the other Nicola why she had neglected to tell her this detail (about the burrowing insect hidden in the grass) *until the final day of their holiday*. The other Nicola confessed that it had slipped her mind (in the midst of a terrifying, ongoing, asiatic hornet infestation). The Author then exfoliated her private parts, vigorously, in the shower.

The two Nicolas also collected a giant haul of quinces from a bush near the motorway services and the scent of these exquisite fruits on the kitchen table has permeated the later stages of *I Am Sovereign*.

Is The Author truly Sovereign?
Is The Author truly Queen of her own Serenity?

On the drive from the ferry terminal, through Calais, the other Nicola kept pointing to the tall, wire fences and adjacent, green patches of ground and telling The Author how on previous visits the entire area had been inhabited by young (for the most part) African men trying to find any means possible of crossing the Channel to Britain. The Author gazed, impassively, at these blank, empty, liminal spaces as they drove by in the other Nicola's little silver Audi TT sports car. Can it be any coincidence then, that only a couple of days later The Author began removing Gyasi 'Chance' Ebo from the narrative?

What does this mean?
For The Author?

What does this mean?
For The Reader?

What does this mean?
For Gyasi 'Chance' Ego ...
No! E-bo! E-bo! E-bo!

The Author wishes The Reader to understand that she has been AT WAR – throughout the entire novella – with auto-correct as a result of the names she has (carefully/blithely) selected for her characters.

Every time The Author writes the name Wang Shu the text is automatically corrected to Wang She. Every time The Author types the name Ying Yue the text is automatically corrected to Ying Due. Every time The Author writes the name Gyasi 'Chance' Ebo, auto-correct instantly tries to alter the surname to Ego. Every time The Author writes the name Avigail, the text is automatically altered to Abigail.

Imagine how The Author has cussed and hissed and growled!
Imagine how The Author has railed against this all-pervasive technological urge to conformity!

The overriding concept for *I Am Sovereign* is that it should take place, in its entirety, during a twenty-minute house viewing in Llandudno. The Author estimates that she has a minute or two left over to play around with. But The Author is determined that this book will be a novella, and every word that she types is extending the length of the novella and thereby transforming it into something bigger and more significant. The novella, as a form, is marvellously unobtrusive. The novella, as a form, is delightfully slight. The novella, as a form, is not too ambitious. The novella, as a form, is eminently manageable. The novella, as a form, is generally unchallenging. The novella, as a form, is unbearably cute. The Author has been prey to 'mixed feelings' about the novel, as a form, ever since completing her last work (*H(A)PPY*) which – to all intents and purposes – destroyed the novel (as a form) for The Author.

How can you continue to live inside a thing that you no longer believe in?
That would be like praying to a God who didn't exist, surely?

No.
No.
I *Am* Sovereign.
The Author just needs to hope. And she needs to love. And she needs to believe, in spite of.

The Author planned – earlier on in the novella – to end the work with Denny Neale (who was then Gyasi 'Chance' Ego) doing a runner with the teddy, and with Ying Due 'borrowing' Charles's late mother's bike and careering into the town on it in hot pursuit.

But this seems all wrong now. The Author can't bear the idea of those four people leaving Charles's tiny work room. They feel so alive to her, all standing there, pushed up, shoved up, close together. There is something so strange, so unlikely, so wonderfully *intimate* about it all.

It dawns on The Author, as she types this, that the room as she describes it (Charles's work room) is exactly like the tiny study in which she herself habitually sits to write. So these four characters are actually here, are they not? In The Author's tiny study, keeping The Author company? The Author has unwittingly brought them here. They are crowding around The Author. Look! They are crashing into her bookshelves, they are poking her with their elbows, they are oppressing her with their demands, they are breathing down her neck. They are bitching and carping and buzzing and rippling and jingling and jangling with their own sweet significance. And The Author loves them all so much, so very dearly, that she cannot bear to say goodbye to them, somehow.